Sherlock Holmes
And The Lyme Regis Trials

†

David Ruffle

Paperback ISBN 978-1-78092-319-2
ePub ISBN 978-1-78092-320-8
PDF ISBN 978-1-78092-321-5

Published in the UK by MX Publishing
335 Princess Park Manor, Royal Drive, London, N11 3GX

www.mxpublishing.com

Cover layout and construction by
www.staunch.com

For Lydia

By David Ruffle

Sherlock Holmes and the Lyme Regis Horror
Sherlock Holmes and the Lyme Regis Horror (expanded 2nd Edition)
Sherlock Holmes and the Lyme Regis Legacy
Holmes and Watson: End Peace
Tales from the Stranger's Room (Editor and contributor)
Tales from the Stranger's Room Vol. 2 (Editor and contributor)

For children

Sherlock Holmes and the Missing Snowman
(Illustrated by Rikey Austin)

Contents

Chapter One

In the spring of 1903 I had every reason to believe myself to be as contented as any man could possibly be. My feelings of contentment came from the bliss of being master of one's own household and I enjoyed nothing better than long evenings spent in the company of my dear wife, Beatrice. My professional life was equally a source of pleasure to me, I had taken over a practice in Queen Anne Street just twelve months before and through the twin attributes of hard work and diligence I had managed to build up this ailing practice into one that now flourished. Beatrice assisted me in this enterprise most ably and I could hardly wish for a better helpmeet. This particular time was also by way of being an anniversary for it was in April of 1902 that we wed, a full six years after our first meeting in Lyme Regis where Mrs Heidler, as she was then, ran a small boarding house. It was a quiet wedding with only a few close friends and family members in attendance including Sherlock Holmes; although he was no lover of marriage as an institution he nevertheless had no objections to serving as my best man on that joyous occasion. This particular cup of contentment of mine was about to run over for on the April morning of which I write, Beatrice informed me that Elizabeth, her daughter-in-law, was expecting a child in late August. Elizabeth was married to Nathaniel, Beatrice's son; they had wed in the spring of 1901 in Lyme Regis, where they still lived. Nathaniel was formerly employed as a boot-boy at the Royal Lion Hotel in the town, but now had settled for the hard, but rewarding life of a fisherman and supplemented the income to be gained from that employment by offering his services locally as a gardener. His mother had hoped he would take over the boarding house that she had run for several years, but when he declined, she presented him with half of the proceeds resulting from the sale of the business, enabling Nathaniel and Elizabeth to begin their life together with no immediate money worries. But I digress; Beatrice was understandably overjoyed to receive the news of approaching parenthood for Nathaniel and Elizabeth.

"Just think," she said, glowing, "I am to be a grandmother."

"And there cannot be one as beautiful as you in the whole country."

"Oh, John, at my age, really?"

"Your age is irrelevant, beauty has not done with you yet, nor I suspect will it ever do so."

"You are too sweet, you really are. Don't forget in your rush to compliment me that you will be a grandfather."

"An honorary one only of course."

"By no means, Nathaniel and Elizabeth will view you as a grandfather as indeed they should, you are family, John. I hope you are not too busy that you cannot get away for a few days for I would dearly love to spend some time in Lyme."

"It will not be easy, but I will see what I can do. Dr Revill owes me a favour or two and this seems like an opportune time to collect one of them."

"Perhaps, Mr Holmes would like to join us; I know how highly he regards Nathaniel."

Holmes had recently taken the decision to retire and despite his proclamations from time to time about the crime to be found in the 'smiling countryside' and his love of the city, he had decamped to the Sussex downs to live a life of solitude and bee-farming. Beatrice was right regarding how highly Holmes thought of Nathaniel even to the point of Holmes making a journey to Lyme for the marriage of Nathaniel and Elizabeth. For Sherlock Holmes, Lyme always brought about mixed feelings; on two previous occasions we had encountered an evil which was at odds with the beauty of the surroundings. All of us, that is to say, myself, Holmes, Beatrice, Nathaniel and Elizabeth had been in mortal peril from two adversaries, one of whom Holmes and I were very familiar with and the other being an opponent other worldly in every possible way. These accounts remain unpublished and will do so for the foreseeable future as no doubt will this particular narrative.

"I will certainly drop him a line, but I have the gravest doubts that he would wish to accompany us, already after such a short space of time he seems completely taken up with this new life of his."

"Appeal to his better nature for, unlike some, I know he has one!"

I duly composed a letter couched in such terms that he might find appealing. When previously in Lyme he had formed a close attachment to the children of my old friend, Dr Godfrey Jacobs and his wife Sarah. The children, Arthur, Cecil and Violet were a little older of course now as seven years had gone by since our first visit to Lyme in 1896, but I was sure they would be pleased to see him and I hoped Holmes would feel the same way.

In the meantime we made our plans; Dr Revill was only too willing to help me out, being assured that I would reciprocate when he needed to be away from his practice. A week after sending my missive to Holmes, I received a reply stating that as the hives had yet to be delivered and his plans to write his volume on 'The Art of Detection' had come to a, temporary he hoped, standstill, he would avail himself of our company and supplied us with a date that happily coincided with the dates we had already chosen for our journey. He further added, 'that as our destination is Lyme perhaps it would be as well for you, my dear fellow, to pack your revolver and I will bring my own choice of weaponry'

Although I was happy that Sherlock Holmes was to join us I could not help, but feel that there was more behind his decision to come than a simple holiday. It was not in Holmes's nature to take trips purely for pleasure, then again he was now retired and undoubtedly had mellowed, so perhaps this was another sign of change in this most remarkable of men. I had not had the opportunity to be of assistance to Holmes very often in the previous two years, our differing professional and personal paths had seen to that, but there were occasions when I was of use to him, even to the point of collecting a bullet for my troubles during the as yet unpublished affair of the, 'Three Garridebs'. The pain I felt from this admittedly minor wound was tempered by my observance of Holmes's usually hidden emotions in turmoil; it gave me a rare glimpse into the heart of the man. As with other cases of this period, I was finding it impossible to

8

afford the time necessary in editing my accounts for publication so at the moment they remain rough drafts for the most part, waiting a time when my busy schedule will allow me the time to put down in print once more, the remarkable exploits of Sherlock Holmes.

The last time that I had spent any appreciable amount of time with Holmes had been in the late summer of 1901 when we found ourselves in Scarborough embroiled in a mystery which although seemingly simple at the outset turned into something darker and more complex.

In the midst of the case I indulged myself at the Scarborough Cricket Festival and had the pleasure of meeting and talking at some length to one of my sporting heroes, Wilfred Rhodes. It was also satisfying to see yet another change in Holmes, for we had encountered two charming and intelligent half-sisters who had set themselves up as consulting detectives. During the course of our investigation Holmes, who had initially poured scorn on their efforts, came to value their abilities. It may well have been a grudging respect such was the man's nature, but respect it was. Miss Poole and Miss Chapman did very well to receive this respect and a measure of approbation, for very few did so, I could testify to that oh so readily!

The arrangement we had put in place was for Holmes to come to us in Queen Anne Street on the day before we travelled so we could get an early start together. Holmes had a surprise for us when he arrived.

Beatrice was in an indecisive frame of mind all day as to what she should feed our guest, for, with Holmes, it was somewhat of a guessing game as to the state of his appetite, not to mention the time of his arrival which was always in doubt. Her concerns were taken away from her upon Holmes's appearance at the door, for he informed us that he had reserved a table for us at Frascati's in Oxford Street. Since opening it had become the talk of the town on account of its opulence and splendour. Fortunately, the cuisine was prepared to an equally high standard.

"This is splendid, Holmes," I said, as I looked around at the most magnificent surroundings. "I might even add that it rivals Scarborough's Grand Hotel."

After we had settled down into our seats on the balcony, I could quite understand that the setting would appear as beautiful as a pantomime transformation-scene to the eyes of any one not blasé by our modern *nil admirari* London. There was gold and silver everywhere. The pillars which supported the balcony and from that, sprang up again to the roof, were gilt and had silver angels at their capitals. There were gilt rails to the balcony, which ran, as in a circus, around the great octagonal building; the alcoves that stretched back seemed to be all gold, mirrors and electric light. What was not gold or shining glass was either light buff or delicate grey and electric globes in profusion, palms, bronze statuettes, and a great dome of green glass and gilding all went to make a gorgeous setting. The waiters in black, each with a silver number in his button-hole, hovered around the tables; somewhere below a string band, which did not in any way impede conversation, played. Sherlock Holmes rubbed his hands gently and smiled genially, observing the grandeur on show while I told the light-bearded manager that what I required was the ordinary table-d'hôte dinner and picked out a *Château Margaux* from the long lists of clarets.

"Mycroft recommended a visit; it seems he was rather taken with it."

"Mycroft?" I queried, "But surely Mycroft goes nowhere out of his own eternal triangle?"

"Come now, Watson, you know very well that even my brother strays occasionally from the set pattern of his life. He has dined here with heads of government departments and indeed the head of the government itself."

"Well, his recommendation is excellent," I commented as I attacked my *Escalope de barbue Chauchat* with a certain amount of gusto.

Both Holmes and Beatrice were feasting on a superb looking *Filets mignon Victoria*, but slowly, as both they and I anticipated the desserts we had ordered from the menu; *Pouding Singapore*, glace vanilla and fromage with fruits. A subdued hum of conversations and the faint rattle of knives and forks against crockery mixed with the music of the band.

10

As we sipped our post-meal port, Holmes explained that his trip to Lyme Regis was not entirely for reasons of pleasure.

"I knew it, Holmes! I thought there was more to your decision than met the eye."

"My deductive processes must be contagious although after twenty-two years it was perhaps time you picked up that particular mantle of mine!"

"The truth is more prosaic; I know you too well, Holmes."

"Have I become such an open book?"

"To some extent, you always have been, even though, paradoxically, I have often been baffled by you, but I am hardly alone in that respect."

"I am sure you are right," chuckled my friend as he reached once more for the port.

"If I may, I will even hazard a guess at the other motive for this trip of yours."

"Please, feel free to do so."

"Or, John, you could just let Mr Holmes tell us himself."

"In just a few moments, he may well have to; I fear my own meagre deductive processes may not be up to this particular challenge."

"We will soon find out, Watson."

I looked around at my now expectant audience, drew in my breath and started.

"I believe dining at this establishment came from a train of thought in your head, unconsciously maybe. I believe you have dined here recently and furthermore, your dinner guest was Mycroft. This would indeed be a rare occasion for you, socialising is not your strong suit, either one of you, so I believe there was business to be discussed and that business involves or requires your presence in Dorset."

"Bravo, Watson. A scintillating deduction."

"Oh, it was quite elementary, my dear Holmes."

"And?" Holmes asked pointedly.

"And what?"

"I believe Mr Holmes needs you to expand a little on your deduction my dear," Beatrice said, with a smile.

"But that's all I have," I said, feeling a little crestfallen.

11

"Never mind, Watson, you have certainly hit upon the starting point in the matter. Now let me apprise you further. I have been asked by Mycroft to sequester myself in Lyme over the next few days and to be an extra pair of eyes and ears."

"For what?"

"Spies, my dear fellow. There is to be a series of tests in Lyme Bay to establish the workability of the latest in submarine warfare, a considerable improvement on the original Bruce-Partington model I am assured. This will no doubt draw many interested observers and amongst those will be some who have rather more than observance on their mind."

"Surely the Admiralty will be able to undertake this function for itself; you are just an individual with limited resources, whereas they can call upon a whole Navy to assist them."

"My resources may be limited, but I assure you my powers are equal to the task," he replied with a huff.

"Apologies, I did not mean to call your skills into question."

"It may well be that my time will be wasted, but even the most insignificant problem, even if it ends with nothing to show for my expertise, would be welcome in these stagnant days."

"But why Lyme Regis? Surely any testing or trialling taking place in the bay may be observed from several vantage points?"

"Indeed so, you are quite correct, but all the dignitaries who are prone to be present on these occasions will be staying in Lyme for the duration of the tests and their observation thereof will be from the end of the Cobb."

"I understand, but it's a shame that your trip to Dorset could not be one of pleasure only."

"I assure you both that seeing young Nathaniel and Elizabeth will be the greatest of incidental delights."

"Tell me, Mr Holmes, if you should chance on any spies or foreign agents, what then?" asked Beatrice as she savoured the last lingering taste of the *Pouding Singapore* on her lips.

"They will be turned over to the appropriate authorities who will decide their fate; they may be deported to their country of origin or tried for treason."

"How can that be? They are not traitorous to their own country. And surely our government sends forth its own spies to foreign lands. No doubt the government's collective voice would be heard if this treatment was met out to our own subjects."

"It's the way of the world when it comes to espionage. I neither condemn nor condone nation's stupidity in this regard, but I do remain fiercely patriotic and as a subject of the realm I endeavour to do my best when called upon," Holmes replied.

"I do not think Beatrice was questioning your patriotism, Holmes, more the whole sorry business of nations seeking to gain ascendancy over others. It reminds me of the time we spent in Scarborough and the ramifications of the Anglo-Japan Alliance, ramifications which brought trouble in its wake six months before it was signed."

"*And* disturbed your cricket watching, Watson!"

"At least this time you are being honest with me about the true purpose of your visit, would that it was so on that previous occasion."

"My secret did not stay hidden from you for long; besides, you had a secret of your own did you not?"

"Only for as long as it took us to get to Kings Cross station!"

In spite of the disapproving glance in my direction from Beatrice, I duly offered my services to Holmes if he indeed needed any assistance.

"Thank you, Watson, but I am hopeful you can enjoy your time in Lyme without being press-ganged into the service of the Admiralty."

"I wonder who would be the hardest taskmaster, yourself or the Admiralty," I said, laughing.

"Perhaps you would care to put it to the test?"

"I think not, better the devil you know as they say!"

The evening ended on a most convivial note and we all repaired to bed anticipating the journey to Lyme the following morning.

It has now been confirmed to this newspaper that the Royal Navy are to maintain a presence in the town whilst trials take place in the bay of a new vessel. We have been given no more information than that and rightly so in our opinion. We understand that some of the most senior officers will be accommodated by the Royal Lion for the duration of these tests. No one at the Royal Lion was available to comment at time of going to press.

Once more, we have nothing to report on the progress being made to open Lyme's railway station. We deplore the interminable delays which hinder and undermine our success as a resort. There are whispers however that August may well see the station fully open. We will see.

Flash floods at the weekend created major concerns for those dwelling in the Jericho area. The river was in full flow from Horn Bridge down to Mill Green, but fortunately the waters receded before any real damage was done.

Chapter Two

Despite Waterloo station being the starting point for so many rail journeys I had undertaken, I was always surprised by just how busy it was, regardless of the time of day I travelled. The noise at times was deafening, a veritable cacophony of sounds that was surely enough to unnerve an unseasoned traveller. Porters, passengers, cabbies and those who made a living selling their wares on the concourse all conspired in this resounding tumult, this assault on the senses.

We had packed as lightly as we were able, being none too sure of how long our sojourn in Lyme would be. Spring in Dorset was prone to bring with it fine weather although I had long since ceased to be reliant on our English weather to behave as predicted. Accordingly we packed outer-wear that would afford us a degree of protection from the south-westerlies that could blow up at any time in Lyme Bay. I, in a moment of weakness or perhaps precognition threw in my old service revolver, much to Beatrice's chagrin. My protestations that it would be useful to have, should Holmes find himself in difficulties, did nothing to ease her worries and I fervently hoped it would reside in the luggage for the duration of our stay in Lyme Regis.

Once we had settled ourselves down in our carriage, Holmes began his now familiar ritual, of reading the morning newspapers from beginning to end, with special scrutiny being made of the agony columns. He had described them to me once as, "a chorus of groans, cries and bleatings….a rag-bag of singular happenings," but also, "the most valuable hunting ground that ever was given to a student of the unnatural." Once that perusal of those columns had been completed,

15

along with the criminal news, then followed another ritual, which was nothing less than the systematic destruction of those papers. It was not unusual to travel with Holmes and find that at the end of our journey there were rolled-up newspapers in every nook and cranny of the carriage.

Having sought permission from Beatrice to do so, Holmes lit his pipe and settled back in his seat.

"Nothing of interest in the papers, Watson," he stated.

"If you say so, I am hardly going to find that out for myself, having neglected to bring an iron with me," I replied, staring pointedly at the balls of paper festooned everywhere.

Holmes dismissed my words with an air of impatience and a wave of his arm in the direction of the remnants of the morning newspapers and puffed at his pipe.

"I take it you mean, 'by nothing of interest', nothing of criminal interest. For all I know, there may be a war being waged, an impending change of government, a national disaster, but as these would fall outside of your purview, they would be banished from your thoughts," I said.

"Precisely so. The events you mention may be of supreme importance to some if not all, but the whimsical happenings that the press fortunately finds the time to report are where life itself is to be found."

"Tell me, Holmes, I know you are eagle-eyed, but surely this mission with which you have been entrusted is rather like looking for the proverbial needle in a haystack."

"Perhaps it is fortunate then that Lyme Regis is not the largest of haystacks!"

"But surely, with high-powered field glasses our spy or spies could observe proceedings from anywhere, such as Thorncombe beacon
in the east to the cliffs atop Branscombe in the west?"

"Quite so, Watson, but I expect that any such agent worth his salt would endeavour to be as close as he could to the heart of the matter which brings us back to Lyme which is, as I have stated, where the top brass of the Admiralty and government will be ensconced. Besides, there may be more than mere observance on the agenda."

"You mean an attempt will be made to steal the plans and suchlike?"

"Or the submarine itself."

"With half the Royal Navy in tow, surely no one would have the audacity to even attempt something so foolhardy."

"There are high stakes to be played for among the nations of Europe, all of whom jockeying for a position of power and dominance so such a move could not be ruled out. We must allow for all eventualities, it has long been an axiom of mine."

"I tend to think you have a thankless task on your hands, Lyme will be full of sightseers who will come from miles around to see these trials."

"Come now, Watson. These trials have not been advertised to the general public like a Punch and Judy show on the beach, the government tends to be a little more circumspect than that, my dear fellow."

"Yes, of course," I replied brusquely, "But all the same, once the trials begin, there will be observers from the general public."

"I concede that point to you, Watson."

"Did the *Bruce-Partington* submarine ever reach the production stage?" I asked.

"It seems there were too many problems for that particular vessel to be pressed into service, although the major part of the design was incorporated into the *Holland-1* the first underwater vessel to be commissioned by the Navy which actually came to some fruition."

"To me, there is something just a little underhand about the use of submarines in warfare. The thought of these machines going about their deadly business, silently under the waves like predatory sharks, fills me with horror," said Beatrice, who had been following our conversation closely albeit with a touch of impatience on her features.

"My dear Mrs Watson, you are not alone in your views. It was not that long ago when Admiral Sir Arthur Wilson expressed similar sentiments calling usage of such vessels, 'underhand, unfair and un-English'. Nevertheless, they are here to stay and will become a vital part of this country's defence strategy."

17

"Do you know the exact nature of these trials, Holmes?" I asked.

"From the information given to me, it appears to be a trial of a new class of submarine, with newer, more powerful battery driven electric motors and an updating of the range of torpedoes and depth charges that can be launched from them."

"So there is no part for the *Holland-1* to play?"

"No, the emphasis is on a new class of vessel, given the designation *A-class*."

"From what little I know of these matters, surely the *Holland-1* is quite new."

"Indeed. She is barely two years old, but already new technology has outstripped her usefulness, besides she was damaged in an explosion a month ago."

"An accident?"

"As yet, the cause of the explosion remains undetermined, but nothing has been ruled out. With these new classes of submarines, Britannia will still continue to rule the waves in spite of the lack of activity on its Navy's part of late. A fact which is of the greatest importance when it comes to outbreak of war."

"I, myself, see no signs of impending war, Holmes."

"I assure you, even now the storm clouds are gathering over Europe and they will not recede or be pacified."

"But, dash it all, most of the Royal families of Europe are related to our own monarch and besides there are so many pacts and alliances in place that one can only think of peace as being the prevailing condition."

"These alliances will be broken, as they have throughout history, as individual nations seek to gain ascendancy over those they may have formerly been in cohorts with. We saw evidence of that, did we not, when we gained some insight into the Anglo-Japan Alliance during our sojourn in Scarborough?"

"Where then do you see this war of yours originating?" I asked.

"The signs tell me that we....."

Holmes got no further with his answer for the signs of impatience I had noticed on Beatrice's features became more

18

pronounced and I realised that she had now had her fill of submarines and the like. She put down one of the newspapers that she had retrieved from the luggage shelf, with a pointed sigh.

"Perhaps, John, we now can talk about *our* reason for visiting Lyme?"

"I am so sorry, Beatrice; you may feel free to blame Holmes!"

"I apportion blame to both of you equally," she said.

"I apologise also," said Holmes, looking for the world as though he actually meant his words. "Rest assured I am looking forward to seeing young Nathaniel and Elizabeth."

"That is as well then, Mr Holmes for they have a request to make of you."

"If I can be of any help to the young couple then I would be only too pleased to be so."

He curled himself up in the rather less than comfortable seat, with his thin knees drawn up to his hawk-like nose and there he sat with his eyes closed, looking to be in a state of extreme languor, but instead, alert and ready for Beatrice's question. With a wave of his arm he bade her continue.

"The question is one that you do not have to answer now for it can be dealt with at a later time, but simply put, Nathaniel and Elizabeth are desirous of you becoming the godfather to their child."

I have rarely seen Holmes so taken aback or indeed momentarily lost for words as he was on this occasion. He shifted uncomfortably in his seat with a look of astonishment on his face. His surprise reflected my own for this request was unknown to me also.

"It is a grand honour they do me in asking, but I fear I am unable to accept. The duty of a godparent as I understand it is to oversee the child's upbringing in the Christian faith; this is something I could not undertake as I don't profess to follow any faith myself nor do I have a belief system which in any way equates to the Christian ideals."

"They are liable to be most disappointed, Mr Holmes."

"Nevertheless, it remains the truth that I cannot fulfil the traditional role of a godfather nor can I stand up in church and make the declaration that is demanded of me. However, I am more than happy to play that role if Nathaniel and Elizabeth wish, but it will have to be in name only."

"A guiding light then?"

"It would certainly be novel to be held up as any kind of example to youth, but I would endeavour to do my best if called upon."

"Thank you, it may be best if you explain it to them in your own words."

"I will certainly do so."

We lapsed into a companionable silence as the train traversed the leafy countryside. The late spring weather had been exceedingly kind to all and sundry after a harsh winter which had seen record low temperatures the length and breadth of the country, with cities and towns grinding to a halt with volumes of snow which could not be removed quickly enough to allow free passage. Commerce had suffered; many shops were forced to close with trade very slow for all manner of retail businesses. It may well be the case that the only people who prospered were coal merchants and doctors. The queues of people outside my surgery door with coughs, colds and sneezes seemed endless and to make matters worse, the coldness of winter gave way to a very wet early spring. Instead of snow and ice, we had in their places, prolonged periods of rain with flooding in those areas that had already been hit the worst in the preceding months. The green meadows and fields we now saw bathed in sunshine, told their own story, the verdant expanses testament to the downpours that we had all endured.

Well over an hour of our journey has passed when I espied the tall, awe-inspiring spire of the Cathedral Church of Saint Mary which signalled our approach into Salisbury station. As we drew slowly into the station I could see the platform was full of people waiting to board or waiting for loved ones to alight.. A few minutes after we had halted a man entered our compartment and enquired as to whether there was a vacant seat available therein. I nodded my assent and he settled himself into the corner. He was a tall man of late middle-age, with greying hair which he wore short and a somewhat crooked mouth which had the effect of throwing his whole face out of balance. He had the appearance of one who had dressed hurriedly and not attended to his toilet properly. I could not rid myself of the feeling that I had met this man, although for the life of me I could not think where or when that may have been. I introduced the three of us to him and took note of his startled expression when he learned he was sharing a carriage with Sherlock Holmes.

I had observed this kind of reaction many times when various folk found themselves in the company of the world's foremost consulting detective. Perhaps they had the notion that Holmes would peer into their very souls with his startling deductions. In spite of our proffering our own names, we did not receive his in return. Whilst we may have deplored his lack of common courtesy, of course we respected his privacy. Our own conversation seemed to be in some way subordinate to our fellow passenger's silence, so at first our conversation was hushed and eventually dwindled away. During the first part of the year there had been high hopes that Lyme Regis would have its own railway station by the spring of 1903, but this was not to be although it was only a few short months later that the station was to open at long last. We gathered our belongings together as the train steamed into Axminster station; our erstwhile companion picked up his valise and scurried out of the compartment without a word.

Nathaniel was there to meet us in person, looking an absolute picture of health. The life of a fisherman may be hard, but there was no doubting the benefits it brought with it. We offered up our congratulations upon his impending fatherhood which caused the poor lad some degree of embarrassment and discomfiture. The early afternoon ride down to Lyme Regis brought us neither sunshine nor rain, but determinedly grey skies which offered up no glimpses of brightness behind the heavy, slow-moving clouds. In spite of Lyme having a somewhat chequered history as far as Holmes and I were concerned, it was still a great joy for me to see the congregated roofs of Lyme and the sea which lapped at the town's edge beyond. The town and its inhabitants had become as familiar to me as any part of London that I had known and Beatrice and I had decided that when I retired we would return and make this beautiful part of Dorset our home. Until that time arrived we endeavoured to spend as much time in Lyme as was possible. Home in spirit, but not in actuality.

The recent spell of very wet weather coupled with the sunshine that has brightened our spirits has brought forth the very real danger of landslips in the area. Residents and visitors are being advised to take extra caution, particularly those who are involved in the delicate operation of prising out fossils from the cliffs. Be vigilant!

The build up of naval shipping in the bay has been most impressive and has quickly become the talk of the town. As we are a town with a proud maritime heritage, we welcome these defenders of our isles.

There is to be a public meeting regarding the museum which still stands empty. This state of affairs cannot be permitted to continue any longer, action must be taken.

Chapter Three

Nathaniel and Elizabeth had managed to purchase for themselves a small cottage in Coombe Street, just fifty yards or so from where Beatrice's guest house had been situated. The dwelling was humble, but homely looking; the interior was cramped and did not allow much natural light to penetrate its rooms yet most importantly they were happy for this was their home, their first home together.

In spite of those cramped conditions they had managed to make enough space to accommodate Beatrice and me for the length of our stay, Holmes had arranged accommodation at the Royal Lion in Broad Street where he was due to meet with figures from the Admiralty that evening.

Elizabeth had brewed some much-needed tea for us and we all arranged ourselves in the tiny parlour. The conversation was animated and for the most part concerned itself with the news we had received. Beatrice looked as radiant as I had ever seen her, her smile and tone infectious to the whole company. Holmes took the bull by the horns and outlined his reasons for having to turn down the offer to be their child's godfather. Nathaniel and Elizabeth took this in good part, understanding precisely just why my friend could not play this role. He assured them however that if there was a role he could play then he would do so. The children of Lyme seemed to have a special resonance for Holmes. He had quickly formed a bond with the children of my old friend, Dr Godfrey Jacobs and his wife Sarah. Arthur and Cecil very soon became favourites with Holmes and although he saw them rarely, nevertheless, the bond was there. When little Violet came along, that bond was extended to include her. He, like me, was fond of Lydia who I had first encountered in the spring of 1896 when her simple philosophy of life was a great comfort during a profoundly difficult time for me. In the years since we had met infrequently, but often memorably, I swear I can still taste the plum pudding she once prepared especially for me during the time she assisted Beatrice with various duties in the guest house.

Nathaniel gave us the latest news regarding friends and acquaintances in the town.

"Sergeant Street and Constable Legg still endeavour to give Lyme a degree of law and order."

"I am sure they succeed," I replied, "They are most able officers. Is Inspector Baddeley still in harness?"

Inspector Baddeley was a police officer Holmes and I had encountered on a few occasions, he was based in the nearby town of Bridport and was entrusted with the investigations into serious crimes when they occurred in this area of Dorset. He was a surly man, unhampered by intelligence or imagination and possessed of an independent attitude which brooked no arguments with his theories and indeed, no assistance.

"Sergeant Street tells me has retired at last," replied Nathaniel, "Perhaps he has taken to studying bees too, Mr Holmes?"

"I sincerely hope not, young man, for the sake of the bees if nothing else!" Holmes replied, "I will no doubt be involved with both Street and Legg over the coming few days."

"What is happening in the bay, Mr Holmes, do you know? There is a large naval presence, the like of which has never been seen here before. There are rumours of course; rumours are the life-blood of the town."

"The Admiralty is testing a new submarine over the next few days, I feel sure I am giving no secrets away by telling you this, for it will become obvious."

"And you have a part to play in this?"

"A small part only, but hopefully a telling one. It has been decided from on high that whatever powers I still possess can be utilised by His Majesty's government in rooting out foreign spies and agents of certain European powers."

"That sounds terribly exciting and dangerous, Mr Holmes," said Elizabeth.

"I fully expect it to be neither, Elizabeth. But it may have the beneficial effect of lifting my life out of the commonplace for a short while before I return to my enforced solitude."

"Come now, Holmes, you protest too much," I interjected, "you positively revel in your new life   and if that ceased to be the case then you could easily return to the life of a consulting detective. Lord knows, Scotland Yard could do with your services, that's for sure."

"You may have a point, Watson. I fear, however, the detectives of Scotland Yard will have to stumble around blindly without me, a skill they have developed admirably."

We continued to discuss life and events in Lyme, there never seemed to be dull times in the town, there was always something happening here, something notable or newsworthy and that had been the case for many hundreds of years. Lyme Regis had never been the kind of community that waited for history to come to it; its role had been the making of history, the partaking in our heritage to the full. Wars, conflicts, politics through the years all left their mark in Lyme or rather it could be said that Lyme left its mark on them.

"Have you had any correspondence from Lydia? I recall you saying, Elizabeth, that she had joined a touring theatre company a while back."

"Yes, that is right, Uncle John, she had the full support of her mother in doing so which is unusual even these days," Elizabeth replied.

"Have you heard how she is finding the theatrical life? Personally, I think she was born to perform so I fervently hope she is making a success of her new life."

Nathaniel laughed, "You will be able to find out for yourself for she has brought a one-woman show to Lyme, written and presented by her, which maps out the life of Mary Anning. It is being performed this week at the Victoria Hall."

"Excellent. Holmes, what say you, will you be able to take in a performance between your patriotic duties?"

"If the chance should present itself to do so then I would be only too pleased to attend."

"I would think the whole town would be only too happy to support a daughter of Lyme in a new venture." I said.

"Not so Mary Anning herself," said Nathaniel.

"Whatever do you mean by that, son?" asked Beatrice.

"It seems Lydia has managed to raise her spectre and the consensus of opinion is that she is not pleased at being portrayed on stage. She has appeared all over the town on various nights, with red, staring eyes and a dreadful look of anger on her face. Superstitious folk in town have taken it to mean her displeasure at Lydia's show."

"And has this had the effect of keeping those folk away from the performances?" asked Holmes, for whom anything out of the ordinary was welcome.

"Far from it, the two shows that have taken place so far have been very well attended, no doubt there have been people curious to see if Mary Anning would attend in person!" answered Nathaniel.

"Has Lydia herself seen this apparent apparition?" Holmes further asked.

"Not that I am aware, she has certainly not mentioned it."

"You would think that if we are indeed faced with an unhappy phantom then Lydia would find herself the object of Mary Anning's haunting appearances rather than the public at large."

"Do I take it, Holmes, that you are giving this story some kind of credence?" I asked.

"Everyone present in this room knows only too well that there are some things which are beyond comprehension, I am sure we are all agreed on that fact."

Holmes's reference was to the supernatural horror that awaited us here on our first visit in the spring of 1896. However, as I have intimated, it is truly a tale for which the world is not prepared, the evil that we encountered on that occasion profoundly affected us all and now we sat there, the five of us in a contemplative mood, remembering with dread those few days when the known world blinked and showed us a hitherto undreamed of abyss of corruption and malevolence.

That mood was shattered along with the window as a stone came hurtling through it with great force, scattering shards of glass throughout the room.

We welcome back a daughter of the town this week; Miss Lydia Hutchings, who it may be recalled left us to try and make her way in the world of the theatre. Evidently, she has made a success of it for she returns to Lyme this week to present a one woman show at the Victoria Hall. It is sure to be well supported for its subject matter is none other than the most famous daughter of Lyme Regis; Mary Anning.

The show is entitled 'The Trials Of Mary Anning' and I am sure the whole town will turn out in force to support Lydia in this venture. The timings of the shows are as yet unconfirmed, but they will be displayed outside the Victoria Hall and in print in our next issue.

A runaway horse caused momentary panic in Broad Street when it bolted and galloped down the street scattering pedestrians in its wake, some of whom received slight injuries as they ran for safety. The horse, Petunia for those who wish to know these things, was recovered in Church Street and was apparently oblivious to the furore it had caused! The animal's owner, Joseph Tesoriere, may well expect a fine for failing to control it.

Chapter Four

Beatrice flew to her son and daughter-in-law and Holmes and I flew to the door. Coombe Street was quiet and without prior knowledge of the direction our stone-thrower had taken we had little or no chance of discovering their trail. We strained hard to see if we could hear retreating footsteps, but all that came to our ears were the occasional calls of seagulls and the insistent lapping of the waves on the beach. We retreated into the house.

Fortunately none of us had been injured by the flying glass although we were extremely shaken by the incident. Beatrice held the offending stone in her hand and wrapped around it, securely fastened by a strap, was a piece of paper which bore the words: Sherlock Holmes-Killer.

"It looks as though one of your foreign agents has decided to make the first move, Holmes."

"It's a possibility my dear fellow, but a supremely unlikely one. Why would anyone wish to draw attention to themselves in this way? Why not just go about their work?"

"Perhaps it's by way of being a warning, Mr Holmes," said a visibly perturbed Nathaniel, "or a threat."

"And yet it appears to be neither, just a plain statement of fact, erroneous I might add. If it is a threat, it is a mighty queer one, don't you think?" he asked of no one in particular.

An idea came to me. "How about Beryl Garcia, I mean Beryl Stapleton as she became? After all you were the one to finally despatch her husband and she was undoubtedly involved in the affair of the Lyme Regis legacy."

"The truth about Stapleton's demise is known only to you, Lestrade, Mycroft and Mrs Watson and by extension, Nathaniel and Elizabeth. I have no doubt she is far away from these shores, living an idyllic life, glad to be free of her domineering and violent husband. I fear we must look elsewhere for both a solution and perpetrator. Who knows, Watson, you may be right and it is the work of one of those men I am to be on the lookout for, but all my senses say otherwise. Let's see what this most singular note may reveal to us."

As Sherlock Holmes studied the note intently, Nathaniel and I effected a hasty repair to the window using some stiff board which would have to suffice until such time as a permanent repair could be made. Elizabeth made another pot of tea to calm our nerves further and we resumed our places around the table.

"Have you gleaned anything from that note, Mr Holmes?" asked Elizabeth as she sipped her welcome tea.

Holmes looked up from his examination of the extraordinary missive. "There are one or two pointers, yes," he replied.

Elizabeth stared at Holmes with an impatient look on her face, "And are you going to share those with us, as we have all been affected by this missile thrown through the window of my house?"

"What? Oh yes, forgive me. The person who penned this is a man of perhaps late middle-age, possibly older. He has worked as a clerk, possibly in a legal context. He is determined, yet of a nervous disposition. He has not been in full employ for some time and uses 'Parisienne' cologne."

"I suppose that rather scuppers my theory of a foreign spy being responsible, eh?"

"It remains the unlikely possibility I formulated a few moments ago, but it is for all that, a possibility still."

"How did you deduce so much from those three words?" asked Nathaniel.

"The fact a man wrote it is obvious from the formation of the letters, male and female approaches to writing are quite distinct. The writing is in an earlier style than that which is common now, giving an indication of his age. You may not be aware that the deduction of a man's age from his writing is one which has been brought to considerable accuracy by experts. In normal cases one can place a man in his true decade with tolerable confidence. He has attempted to disguise his copperplate style of writing, but not wholly successfully; it is a form most used by clerks, particularly those who work for barristers and solicitors. Determined, simply because he carried this action through. The fact he was nervous can be deduced by the tell-tale white spots on the paper which are owing to perspiration from his hands as he penned this note. The paper is of the finest quality, but has been allowed to dry out and rendered almost unusable, surely it is not too much of a leap of imagination to deduce a loss of income, although there is a possibility that he has borrowed this paper from another source where it had been left to mellow, shall we say, with age. The cologne is obviously deduced by the lingering smell of it on the paper. There are seventy-five perfumes, which it is very necessary that a criminal expert should be able to distinguish from each other and cases have more than once within my own experience depended upon their prompt recognition. There are one or two more trifling indications, but these will suffice."

Nathaniel leaned back in his chair, fingers steepled together in the manner of Holmes himself, "Now if you could only give us the name of this man 'we poor old policemen would be very, very grateful, sir'."

We all laughed at this interjection from Nathaniel. Humour is a great antidote for the trials of life and can be found at the strangest of times and in the oddest of circumstances.

"Will you be informing Sergeant Street of this incident, Holmes?"

"As there is so very little to report, I think not. All that is required is a certain amount of vigilance on my part."

"And ours, Holmes."

"Thank you, my friends. I think I should take myself off to the Royal Lion and meet with my paymasters."

I glanced at Beatrice, a little unsure of my ground. She, who knows me so well, nodded her assent to my unspoken question.

"I will stroll along with you, Holmes, I feel in need of a little air."

"Transparently, that is not the case, but I would be grateful for your company all the same."

The Royal Lion was just a few minute's walk away and as we walked Holmes informed me who he was expecting to see at this meeting.

"It is my belief that Lord Walter Kerr will be there in person."

"You say the name as though I should be aware of it, but I assure you I am not."

"There is no especial reason why you should unless you have happened to see his name mentioned in 'The Times' or 'The Daily Telegraph'. He is the First Naval Lord, in effect the Admiral of the Fleet."

"High matters of state indeed then."

"Certainly, high matters of the Royal Navy, Watson."

As we turned the corner into Broad Street I glanced across at the Assembly Rooms, there were a few early evening visitors crossing its portal. Somehow, the rooms seemed out of place, out of time and I had my doubts that the building would survive many more years before it was demolished in the name of modernity and progress. The advent of the motor-car had begun to change the roads and streets of our towns; it would come as no surprise to me to find that this fine building would be torn down in the future to provide a space where people could park their contraptions. Too much of our heritage is razed to the ground with so little regard for our proud history. Perhaps Lyme Regis would be the exception to this wholesale destruction and who knows, the Assembly Rooms may survive intact.

I could see a poster adorning the side of the Victoria Hall, which adjoined the Assembly Rooms. I crossed to the other side of the road for a closer look. It was hand-drawn and hand-coloured and advertised the merits of Lydia's one woman show, 'The Trials of Mary Anning'. The title of the drama puzzled me momentarily, my mind was automatically drawn to see trials as criminal trials and for the life of me I could not recall any such event in the life of Mary Anning, the palaeontologist and fossil hunter of Lyme. I then realised that her trials were those of a woman working in a field where men were pre-eminent and how hard she had to work to gain the respect she did in the scientific world. She even suffered legal discrimination as she was of religious dissenting stock who were not looked on with any great favour. The family remained poor and she suffered the loss of her father when she was just eleven years of age. Trials enough one would think.

At first glance I imagined the drawing on the poster to be depicting Mary Anning herself, but a closer examination revealed it to be Lydia in her stage persona, wearing a bonnet, long dress and carrying a fossil hammer with a bag slung over her shoulder for the fossil finds to be placed in. Perhaps Mary Anning objected to this appropriation of her likeness and had come back from the grave with vengeance in mind! What nonsense I thought, what ineffable twaddle.

When we reached the Royal Lion just a few moments later I bade Holmes good evening and turned to go.

"Are you not staying, Watson? I am sure the good Mrs Watson can spare you for a short time."

"I am not at all sure my presence will be required by the Admiralty."

"Possibly not, but I assure that *I* would welcome your presence, however if you wish to return to your family I will understand," he said, head bowed.

It was difficult to refuse any of Sherlock Holmes's requests, for they were always so exceedingly definite and put forward with such a quiet air of mastery. The passage of years had not altered this. I have always had such a deep respect for the extraordinary qualities of the man that I have always deferred to his wishes, even when I least understood them.

"Very well, Holmes, if you feel that I can be of any help to you in this matter."

"Excellent, Watson. It makes a considerable difference to me as you know, having someone with me on whom I can thoroughly rely. Local aid, should I choose to avail myself of it, is always either worthless or biased."

"That rather denigrates Sergeant Street and Constable Legg does it not? They are most able officers and have been of the greatest help to us in the past," I replied, somewhat indignant on their behalf.

It was one of my friend's most obvious weaknesses that he was impatient with less alert intelligences than his own. I, above all could identify with that trait of the man, being the recipient of perhaps many hundreds of withering glances and barbed comments through my long years of association with Holmes.

"You are right to be indignant, Watson, I feel my words were a little too hasty. I do have the greatest of respect for those two local upholders of the law and rest assured if I feel they can be of any aid to us then I will call on them," he said, as he pushed open the door and entered the hotel.

The instant we entered, Holmes was approached by a young, slightly nervous looking man wearing the uniform of a second lieutenant. He flashed a hesitant smile at Holmes and ignored my presence altogether.

"You are Mr Sherlock Holmes?" he asked in a somewhat hesitant manner.

"I am he," replied my friend, "and you are?"

"Lieutenant Matthew Webb at your service, sir. I have instructions to take you up to the Admiralty suite where the First Sea Lord and other senior officers await your presence."

"The Admiralty suite? Has the Royal Lion become a maritime hotel in my absence?"

"Oh no, sir, at least I don't think so," Webb replied with growing confusion apparent on his features. "It's been named that because the Admiralty have taken over a suite of rooms on one of the upper floors of the hotel. I am not sure if that suite actually has a name, sir. I mean to say, that it may have, but not with a maritime connection, although it could have I suppose. I could find out for you, sir."

"That will not be necessary, Lieutenant Webb, if you would just escort us in accordance with your instructions that will be aid enough," Holmes replied.

The light seemed to dawn on the lieutenant that the 'us' referred to by Sherlock Holmes alluded to the patient man standing by his side.

"I was only asked to wait for *you* and take *you* to see the Naval Secrets Committee, sir." He coughed and spluttered in a most un-officer like manner, "I may have said too much in a public area such as this; the Naval Secrets Committee is a highly secret gathering."

"Thank you, Webb," said Holmes, with a little amusement in his voice, "I had deduced as much."

34

"What? Oh yes, sir, I see. The point is that my orders did not refer to a colleague of yours and if I follow those orders to the letter than I am unable to admit your friend to the Admiralty suite. Although I suppose I could dash up the stairs and ask whether it would be in order, but that may be seen as a weakness on my part in not following express orders I have been given, but on the other hand it could be perceived as showing initiative. What do you think, sir?"

"I think we could be having this rather pointless and wearisome conversation for the rest of the evening unless you or we take positive action. So, lay on, Macduff!"

"Pardon? Oh, Shakespeare. Very well, gentlemen, follow me."

With a despairing shake of the head from Holmes in the direction of Webb's fast disappearing back, we followed our welcoming lieutenant to an upper floor of the hotel. Webb stood to attention outside the first door we came to, even before knocking. He rapped loudly on the door. The door opened immediately and I caught sight of another uniformed man as the smell of cigar smoke wafted into the corridor.

"Mr Sherlock Holmes, sir," announced Webb.

"Thank you Lieutenant. Who is the other gentleman?" asked the as yet nameless officer.

"Sir, he is a friend or colleague of Mr Holmes, or possibly both I suppose."

"His name, Webb, his name?"

"I have not asked, sir," replied the hapless Webb.

"Then please do…"rejoined the uniformed man and then with an audible sigh changed his mind as to what he was going to say and simply said, "Lieutenant Webb, you may stand down for now."

"Thank you, sir," Webb saluted, turned and disappeared from view.

"I am Richard Elkin, attached to the Admiralty for the duration."

"Allow me to introduce Doctor John H Watson, who as you may know, has been of the utmost assistance to me during my career."

35

"Good evening, Dr Watson. It's a little irregular, Mr Holmes, we expected to have dealings with only you and we are discussing very confidential matters here tonight."

"Dr Watson is the very soul of discretion and his keeping of confidences is a byword in his life." Holmes said, on my behalf.

"Be that as it may, Mr Holmes," came a booming voice from the innermost depths of the room, "it is the intention of the Admiralty and therefore me to deal with you and you alone. I am sure that acting on this knowledge, Dr Watson will be good enough to withdraw and leave us to our deliberations. Mr Holmes, you have an official standing, in no small part owing to the influence of your brother, but I will not allow all and sundry to become a part of this matter."

"Lord Walter Kerr I presume," stated Holmes and held fast on to my sleeve for I had made my mind up to withdraw and was turning towards the door as Holmes spoke, "May I stress to you that Dr Watson is no stranger where matters of high state are concerned and has been of the utmost assistance to me in cases brought to us by various members of previous governments of this nation. His discretion is assured and I regret to say I will not be able to aid you unless Dr Watson is by my side."

Lord Walter Kerr glanced at his fellow committee members for support, but as one they all looked down at their feet and left the First Sea Lord to take Sherlock Holmes on alone. His features remained hardened for what seemed an eternity until he relaxed somewhat and leaned back in his chair, sighed deeply and looked Holmes in the eye.

"Against my better judgment, Mr Holmes, I accede to your request."

He proceeded to introduce us to the other members of the committee, namely, and as far as I could ascertain, in descending order of importance; Admiral John Chamberlain, Captain Henry Fortescue, Mr Silas Browning and Richard Elkin who had greeted us at the door.

Richard Elkin now addressed Holmes, "You have no doubt been made aware by your brother Mycroft of the importance of these trials and the future benefit to this nation. You may even think your

36

task is an impossible one and perhaps it is, but we are assured that you are the very best man for this mission."

Holmes nodded curtly and motioned Elkin to continue.

"I have papers here which list certain agents who may be players in this game of ours, those who seek out secrets and sell them to the highest bidders. Enemies of the state no less."

"The men on the list," and here Holmes produced his own copy from the depths of his inner pocket, "do not see themselves as enemies of the state for they have no state they owe allegiance to, their allegiance is to money and the pursuit of it. They act for gain, not glory."

"Be that as it may, Mr Holmes, their acts from our standpoint would be construed as treason. Are you familiar with these names?"

Holmes put the list into my hands and said, "Yes, I still follow reports of continental crime and my brother is always on hand to keep me abreast of all that happens outside my purview that he thinks may be of interest to me. I have taken the liberty of adding two names of my own to my brother's inventory."

The names on the list, all unknown to me, were: Paolo Campini, Meredith Eccles, Giorge Marantz, Jacob Lowenstein and Sebastian Morland. The next long minutes were spent in detailing recent movements of these men and an appraisal of how likely they were to be involved in plots of this nature. Arguments were presented back and forth across the table with lightning speed until my head began to spin and I came to thoroughly regret my decision to accompany Holmes to the Royal Lion. I did have a question of my own however.

"Excuse me gentlemen, but if the Admiralty is so apprehensive about losing the plans to the new A-class submarine, why are they here at all? Why are they not locked up in a Whitehall safe?"

Captain Fortescue let out an audible sigh, such as a teacher might use when displaying impatience towards a slow child.

"The plans have to be present at the trials for the purposes of reference and also for that of alteration or modification if need be. It would be dashed impossible to trial the submarine without the physical presence of the plans."

"Thank you," I replied and hoped my tone conveyed my apologies for what must have seemed to them a pointless question. Other questions occurred to me, but I kept my own counsel on them. I fear I may have drifted, thus putting me in an unfavourable light, for the next voice I heard was Holmes and the meeting appeared to have moved on.

"The threat from these five men is tangible enough, but only in respect of obtaining the plans or blueprints of this vessel. To actually make away with the submarine itself is not a game they would care to play so we are left with unspecified agents who work directly for European powers who may have been planning such a move for many long months."

"Regardless of our fears, Mr Holmes," said Elkin, "this strategy of having the trials take place in Lyme Bay has only been announced to the various heads of staff and the officers involved. I seriously doubt any of these powers that may oppose us or seek to gain an advantage would have had the time necessary to mount such an operation, but your presence here shows that we do have very real concerns in that direction."

"The timing of the announcement has no bearing on the matter for the planning has been long in the making and it is obvious that even the best kept secrets of government are apt to fall into the wrong hands. Even now, gentlemen, you have spies of your own spread out over the continent gathering information clandestinely. Now, as to whether anybody would be foolhardy enough to attempt such an operation, well, that is another question entirely," said Holmes.

I interjected, "With the might of the Royal Navy attending I see no way such a coup could possibly succeed, whatever the power, whatever their resources."

"The might of the Royal Navy on this occasion will consist of a handful of ships only, Dr Watson, but I do take your point," replied Chamberlain, who had been silent until now.

"I can think of at least seven separate scenarios whereby such an audacious scheme may succeed," said Holmes imperiously.

I felt compelled to speak once more, "Is having the balance of power so very important after all? Has any nation ever been in a position to avert a war because they were deemed to be a stronger nation or had superior strengths, be it navy or army? Have we, Great Britain, the divine right to seek to control the rest of Europe?"

"We do not seek to control, Dr Watson nor to dominate, but to help maintain the increasingly fragile peace. If we can do this diplomatically then all well and good, but if necessary it will have to be by a show of force. If I may say so, Doctor, your words do not speak to me of the patriot I imagined you to be," replied Chamberlain.

"The paradox is that you seek to maintain this peace by producing a new and formidable vessel with increased weaponry and killing power. I assure you I am indeed a patriot; I served my time during the Afghan wars and have never stinted in my service for Queen and country, but I am also a pragmatist and seeing firsthand the horrors of war does tend to make one think very forcibly of the alternatives that may be available in bringing such conflicts and disputes between nations to an end."

"We are pragmatists, we are realists and the reality is that war can more easily be avoided if one nation is perceived to be stronger, it acts as a mighty deterrent," said Silas Browning

"History shows us that that is just so much nonsense, Mr Browning," said Holmes, entering the affray, "if there were a grain of truth in it then wars would be a thing of the past surely."

"Ah, but some nations are not merely content to hold a balance of power to keep or maintain a peace; instead they seek to dominate smaller countries to further their own predominance," retorted Browning.

"One could make that remark regarding the British Empire, Mr Browning," said Holmes.

"I am sure it will be possible for all nations to live in peace at some time in the future," I said, more in hope than expectation.

"Or shortly thereafter," added Holmes philosophically.

Kerr had been sitting back in his chair with a resigned look while these exchanges were flowing across the room. That resignation disappeared as he stood up and brought his fist crashing on to the table.

"Gentlemen, gentlemen. Can we please adhere to the matter at hand? This is not a debating chamber. Mr Holmes, in view of your comments and those of Dr Watson, who may I remind you is here under sufferance, do you still wish to undertake this commission on behalf of your country?"

"Even allowing for my misgivings, I am, as the good doctor stated himself to be, a patriot and if you think my powers are equal to the task then I undertake to perform it to the best of my ability."

"Thank you, Mr Holmes. Is there anything more you need from us tonight?"

"I believe I have all I need. Am I to report to you in person or the committee as a whole?"

"Initially to Mr Elkin who will evaluate your information, should there be any of course, and then he will make the decision as to whether the material should be placed before all of us."

Our business concluded for the evening, we said our good-nights and made our way downstairs. The bar looked a very welcome sight indeed, but I was conscious of my duty towards Beatrice. Holmes stared at me pointedly.

"Just one surely, Watson?"

I acquiesced; perhaps it may be said, rather too easily.

Your humble scribe was fortunate to be present at the opening night of 'The Trials Of Mary Anning', the show brought to us by former Lyme resident, Miss Lydia Hutchings. It was a delight from start to finish. Miss Hutchings played all the parts which included Mary herself, the Philpot sisters, William Buckland, Henry De La Beche and many more. Her rapid changes of costume were accomplished with the speed that you may be accustomed to seeing by quick-change artistes at the varieties. I offer the heartiest of congratulations to Lydia for this thoughtful and entertaining show. A word of praise too, for her brother Anthony, who was responsible for the lighting and props, both of which were perfect.

As the holiday season approaches we encounter yet again the perennial problem of whether or not to allow dogs onto our beaches. For the town council this seems to be an insoluble and thorny problem. Our view is simple...no dogs!

Chapter Five

We settled ourselves down into comfortable corner seats in the dimly lit yet atmospheric bar, with a brandy and soda each. The general hubbub of conversation went on around us, the clinking of glasses, laughter and general bonhomie.

"I fear I may have strained somewhat the patience of your paymasters, Holmes."

"You have every right to say what you feel, they may wish to call on our bodies, but they cannot do the same with our consciences, our beliefs."

"Do you believe that any of these men on your list, Paolo Campini, Meredith Eccles, Giorge Marantz, Jacob Lowenstein and Sebastian Morland will actually put in an appearance?"

"Well remembered, Watson! I have my doubts; it is far too public a stage for them I believe."

"Does that apply to the names you added yourself, whoever they are?"

"Sorry to keep you in the dark, Watson. They are Charles Leclerc and Hans Sulzbach, two newcomers to the game if you like, but both equally capable of playing for the highest stakes."

"I cannot for the life of me see how the Admiralty can expect you to locate any or all of these men. Should they not be concentrating their own resources into this task?"

"Perhaps they have been misled by my brother into thinking I have skills over and above those of mere mortals," he replied with a wry smile. "I have my dossier, I have my sheaf of notes and my photographs and who knows; we may yet ensnare one of these avaricious hirelings."

"I still say that the analogy of a needle in a haystack holds true."

"I also have a secret weapon of my own, Watson; it may not have the potency of the Navy's torpedoes, but will have an effectiveness of its own."

"And what may that be?"

"My Lyme Regis Reserves, more mature than the wild, but efficient Baker Street Irregulars. These reserves will be armed with all the information that I now possess, so you see our little force of two now becomes multiplied and becomes a capable organisation."

"Am I being dense here, Holmes? I have never heard of the Lyme Regis reserves. Do I take it you mean Sergeant Street and Constable Legg?"

"And you of course, Mrs Watson, Nathaniel, Elizabeth, Dr Jacobs and Sarah, Arthur, Cecil, perhaps even Lydia. You can all become my eyes and ears."

"Only if they have a mind to and I am not happy about Beatrice being so conscripted, I will not have her subject to danger."

"My dear fellow, there is no conscription involved or danger I hasten to add. All I ask of everyone is to see and observe and if Mrs Watson chooses not to become a reserve then of course I will not press the issue."

A clearly off duty Lieutenant Webb approached us at that juncture, a glass of beer in his hand. Even out of uniform he looked every inch the lieutenant he was.

"I hope all went well with the Naval Secrets Committee, gentlemen? I mean the Admiralty suite."

"Yes thank you Lieutenant Webb," I replied for both of us. "But don't let us keep you," hoping he would take the hint.

"Well, if I can be of any help, please feel free to call upon me. Of course, I am here to help you officially, but I meant unofficially when I said what I said, just now I mean. I hope that is clear to you gentlemen."

"As the deep, blue sea," I replied, "Goodnight, Lieutenant."

Lieutenant Webb ambled off in the direction of the counter, but before our conversation could continue anew we had another visitor. Constable Legg, a policeman of some year's service in Lyme. He was rather excitable early on in his career, but had become stolid and dependable and the ideal foil for Sergeant Street who he obviously looked up to.

"Good evening, Dr Watson, Mr Holmes. I trust you are both well?"

"Hullo, Legg. We are both very well thank you and I trust we find you in the same condition?"asked Holmes..

"I am very well also, thank you, Mr Holmes."

"And how fare the criminals of Lyme?" I asked in a light-hearted fashion.

"They don't give us much trouble on the whole, Doctor. They know us and we know them, it's the visitors you have to watch out for, present company excepted of course!"

"There appears to be a few of those amongst you at the moment," I said, motioning towards the counter where a few naval types were talking animatedly.

"Oh well, they seem harmless enough and besides if they do step out of line, why then, the navy can deal with its own. I doubt if any of them would stoop to the petty vandalism that I have suffered tonight."

"What was that, Constable Legg?" asked Holmes, his senses heightened by the merest mention of anything out of the ordinary.

"Nothing to worry you with, Mr Holmes, just some scamp threw a stone through my window earlier, fair put the wind up me for a minute I can tell you."

Holmes leaned forward, his eager face wearing an expression of intense and high-strung energy which showed me that some novel and suggestive circumstance had opened up a stimulating line of thought. Even I could see that there was here, a coincidence that demanded further investigation. Holmes's words however betrayed none of this.

"There are always lunatics about, Legg; indeed it would be a dull world without them. Tell me; was there a message or note attached to this stone?"

"A message, sir? How do you mean?"

"A note for instance, fastened to the stone. Was there nothing like that at all?"

"No sir, it was just young lads having a bit of fun at my expense I reckon. I do have an idea who it might be and I will make sure they pay."

Just then, there was a certain amount of commotion in the furthest corner of the lounge whose large windows looked out onto the street. There was scream or two then voices raised. We heard disconnected voices: *'It was her.' 'Mary Anning.' 'Looked just like her picture.' 'Oh my God, those eyes'* Those who had been congregated in that part of the lounge now moved as far away from the windows as they could. *'She looked straight the window at me. I have never seen a face like it.'* was a further comment that reached our ears.

On hearing the commotion Legg had begun to gravitate towards the source of the pandemonium, but on hearing the raised voices, retraced his steps and dashed outside. He came back a few moments later, sweat glistening on his brow.

"All clear out there now," he said, to the assembled throng, some of whom were being calmed down by both the staff and complementary brandies.

He sat down with us. "Have you heard this talk about the ghost of Mary Anning? It is reckoned by some superstitious folk hereabouts that her spirit has been raised in annoyance at the portrayal of her life that is being performed at the Victoria Hall. Nonsense I say, but some people would believe anything. I reckon it's just someone having their fun, although I think it may have cost the Royal Lion a few shillings in brandies tonight. Whoever it is, I'll catch them and they will be the ones scared to death when I've finished with them. Well, that's enough excitement for me tonight; I'll be off home, gentlemen."

"We'll walk with you, Constable."

"To protect me from ghosts and ghoulies?" he laughed.

"Hardly that," Holmes replied, "more to satisfy a certain curious streak in me that manifests itself whenever odd happenings occur."

"I didn't know you paid any credence to the supernatural, Mr Holmes."

"The odd happenstance I refer to is actually the hurling of the stone which was thrown through the window of your house."

"But that was nothing, sir, like I said. Just a local lad or two playing a prank, probably those lads I caught in Mr Sage's orchard. I don't see that it would be of any interest for you, Mr Holmes."

"Holmes has had the same....." that was as far as I got with my explanation of Holmes's interest in the matter before the stern look I received stopped me in my tracks. To cover my confusion I mumbled some nonsense until Legg returned his attention to Sherlock Holmes.

"Nevertheless, Constable Legg, I would like to see the scene of the crime, if I may term it as such, for myself."

We donned our coats and ventured outside into Broad Street. The darkness surprised me as did the lateness of the hour. All was quiet at the Victoria Hall; Lydia's performance tonight must have long come to an end. We did not have far to walk for Legg lived in Charmouth Road, just a few hundred yards away from the Royal Lion. There was dampness in the air, a mist sitting over the town like a protective blanket, clinging to the buildings blurring both shape and form. The town had an atmosphere all of its own quite unlike any other town I had ever visited and the presence of so deep a mist served only to heighten that atmosphere, giving Lyme an aura of mystery and rendering it a place where it was easy to believe that anything could happen. On such nights it was not difficult to imagine shades of the past walking alongside the corporeal beings of the present. I would not have been astonished in the slightest to find Mary Anning walking along with us on such an evening. Notwithstanding that, I still shuddered as we walked past St Michael's churchyard which is her resting place.

John Legg lived with his mother in a cottage which managed to somehow look pristine even in the ink-black of the night.. The board over one of the windows rather detracted from that view however. Sherlock Holmes asked Legg if he had a lantern which could be pressed into service and also asked him to apologise to his mother for our intrusion into her tidy front garden.

"No need to worry on that score, Ma is away for a few days in Northamptonshire so I have a little time to get the place shipshape again."

"The sweeping up of the glass should be an easy enough task," I commented.

"There is also the cleaning and ironing to be dealt with and a spot, well, more than a spot of general tidying up. I never seem to have the time for such jobs," Legg sighed, failing utterly to convince us.

He brought out his bulls-eye lantern which he kept for official duties and handed it to Holmes who was peering at the ground below the window. After a few moments spent in scrutinising the area aided by the light of the lantern, he stood up and exclaimed.

"Here it is; a little damp, but still decipherable."

"What is it, Holmes, a note?" I asked.

"Yes indeed, Watson, but it was not attached to the stone firmly enough to survive its flight."

"What does it say?"

By way of an answer he straightened out the piece of paper and shone the light upon it, enabling us to see the most singular message written on it: `John Legg-Killer`.

There seems to be mass hysteria present in the town at the moment, we can describe it in no other terms. It has been reported that the spectre of Mary Anning has been seen. Variously reported as displaying a sad or sometimes angry countenance or even malevolent according to some. These appearances have been attributed to Mary's displeasure at the portrayal of her by Miss Lydia Hutchings in her delightful show.

These spurious reports feed off each other, becoming more sensational in the telling and re-telling. It is our view and the view of many God-fearing folk in the town that these witnesses are mistaken in what they see. The latest incident occurred at the Royal Lion yesterday evening when a large number of people would be willing to swear that 'Mary Anning' gazed through the window at them in a threatening manner.

It is to be hoped that this hysteria will disappear as quickly as it has arisen. A happy by-product of all this for Lydia is that ticket sales have increased two fold.

Chapter Six

I had always thought, and indeed still do so, of Lyme Regis as a town and resort with something for everyone, but an evening of stone-throwing, disturbing messages, ghosts and talk of spies and secret agents was perhaps stretching that thought a little too far!

Constable Legg was completely bewildered by this turn of events.

"A killer? What does that mean- a killer?" he asked in a most agitated manner as we were sitting around the small table in the kitchen. "I have never killed anyone, not a single living creature. This is not my idea of a prank; there will be hell to pay for this."

"You still see this as a jape of sorts then?" asked Holmes.

"How else can I see it?" rejoined the hapless Legg.

Sherlock Holmes then related to Legg how he too had been the recipient of such a missile and message earlier in the evening.

"I see now why you reject the idea of it being a prank, but I am still mystified why anyone would do such a thing and why?"

"We have very little data to work with I am afraid and who knows, it may yet turn out to be a form of high-spirited jape," Holmes stated, but the look on his face told me he thought otherwise.

"But, Holmes, no one could have had foreknowledge of your arrival here."

"Not quite so, Watson, certain members of the Admiralty staff would have certainly known of it."

"You are surely not suggesting that any of those worthy people may be involved in this?"

"Not at all. However, it remains true that whoever directed that stone through Nathaniel's window knew of my presence before my actual arrival or at the very moment of it," Holmes stated categorically.

"I am not quite with you on this talk of Admiralty staff, gentlemen. I know of course that there are some kinds of trials taking place, but the local constabulary have been told to go about their normal business and not to become involved in any way with the proceedings."

"I propose to put both yourself and the sergeant in the picture tomorrow morning. Shall we say ten o' clock at the home of Nathaniel Heidler? I assume you know the address?"

"Yes, Mr Holmes. I will speak to Joe, I mean Sergeant Street, in the morning. Do you wish me to tell him of the incident involving yourself and our stone-thrower?"

"If you wish to do so then certainly, it can do no harm and may in fact do some good."

We wished Legg good-night and Holmes departed for the Royal Lion where he would be sequestered for the duration and I back to Coombe Street much later than anticipated.

Beatrice, Nathaniel and Elizabeth were still up and conversing when I entered the house. I sensed a degree of merriment in their enquiries as to how my evening had been spent, particularly after the smell of brandy had been detected on my breath. It took the form of a firing squad making sport with their captive. I decided to stick to the plain facts; if my future were black it was better surely to face it like a man than to attempt to brighten it by mere will-o'-the-wisps of the imagination. Any discomfiture I felt with regards to being out so long disappeared as I rendered my now rapt audience with an account of my evening, being careful to gloss over those moments when I may have drifted into occasional slumber. They were intrigued and horrified to hear of the attack on John Legg's house or to be more accurate, Mrs Margaret Legg's house.

"Does Mr Holmes have any idea why he and John should have been singled out this way?" asked Beatrice.

"If he has, he has not seen fit to enlighten me," I replied, somewhat testily. "The list of possible culprits can be shortened to those who knew that Holmes would be here, but at this stage he does not know who precisely would be on such a list."

"It might have been a spur of the moment crime that only happened because this man, whoever he may be, spotted Mr Holmes entering this house," opined Nathaniel.

"That may well be so, but that takes us no further in identification of the perpetrator or the connection between Constable Legg and Holmes, two men whose paths have rarely crossed," I stated. "On the other hand it may be that this particular person's crime spree has reached its apogee with these two acts of aggression and that is all we will hear from the man."

I outlined Holmes's plan to re-invent the Baker Street Irregulars as the Lyme Regis reserves to hopefully render him useful assistance by the way of extra ears and eyes. I expected the reaction to this proposal to be muted, but was surprised by the positivity displayed. Everyone wanted to do their bit. It was agreed we would all be ready for Holmes the next morning at ten where he would tell us what he required of us. I assured them that the task would not be too onerous.

The next morning dawned bright and clear and, not quite on a whim, and as the household was still slumbering, I decided to walk towards the sea with a view to taking an early morning swim. I had mentioned to Nathaniel before we retired that I was quite struck with the idea of a sea immersion to start my day and he was good enough to find for me a swimsuit of his own that I could borrow. It was a tight fit, but with a struggle I managed to get into it. It was a fresh morning and after only a few steps I was almost regretting my decision, but the sight of the sea changed all that. There was a slight breeze which danced across the surface of the water throwing up the odd ripples as opposed to fully-formed waves. I removed my boots on the cart road and made my way across the shingle. The sun had not yet risen and the pebbles which made up the beach were as cold as night and extremely difficult to negotiate; I feared I must have looked a madman to anyone observing my haphazard route across the shingle. I laid my trousers and jacket down a few feet from where the sea was lapping at the edge of the beach. When the water lapped over my feet it had the immediate effect of taking all feeling away from my toes, once again weakening my resolve. I decided if I was going to take the plunge both figuratively and literally then I should just press on forthwith. A bold move seemed to me to be the best gesture and to that end I walked purposefully to the end of the jetty and with barely a second's pause dived straight in.

I knew just how cold the sea would be, but all the same it swamped my senses, drawing the breath from my body involuntarily. Paradoxically, it felt as though my body was on fire as I immersed myself fully beneath the slight waves, the sensations it caused rampaged through my body, but calmed down as I began to swim away from the shore. It was then that I felt that inner peace that comes to me whenever I have swam in the ocean. I drifted, swam and drifted a little more on the gentle peaks of the waves. Twenty or so minutes had passed thus when I kicked out for the shore with a now ravenous appetite for the breakfast that would await me.

As I dried myself as best I could, another early morning swimmer approached. He was a fairly tall man, distinguished looking although that look was somewhat compromised by the garish yellow headgear he carried with him which he proceeded to place on his head. I thought uncharitably that it could also be used as a warning buoy for I felt sure that it would be visible to shipping the length and breadth of the English Channel!

"Good morning," he said, with a pronounced Scottish accent and the slightest trace of another which I could not identify.

"Good morning to you too," I replied, "And what a lovely morning it is too. My name is Watson, Doctor John Watson."

"Very pleased to meet you, I have seen you from time to time in the town of course. Hugh Duncan, how are you?" he asked, gripping my hand firmly.

"Sir Hugh?"

"The same, but although I tend to wear my knighthood lightly my fame, such as it is, is appears to have preceded me."

"Only in a manner of speaking; I encountered your name a few years ago when Sherlock Holmes and I investigated a series of murders here which revolved around the inheritance known as the Twynham legacy of which you were the beneficiary."

"Yes, I recall the excitement still present in the town when I returned from a business trip I had undertaken to South Africa."

52

"An auspicious trip for you, for your life would certainly have been in danger had you been in Lyme at the time."

"So I understand. Still here I am, safe, sound and raring to go on my morning swim."

"Yes of course, don't let me keep you, Sir Hugh. It was good to meet you."

"And you too, Doctor Watson."

Fortified by my swim I walked back to Coombe Street with the gait of a righteous and virtuous man. Elizabeth was the only one up and I gave her some assistance in the preparation of breakfast. Gradually, the rest of the household stirred and just in time for we had laid out the breakfast wares in the small parlour a few moments before.

The talk over our meal was of the attack on John Leggs's house. We were all struck by the singular nature of this assault, an assault which had no rhyme or reason to it for none of us could think of any circumstance whereby Legg could possibly be termed a killer. Our conversation also ranged over the forthcoming naval trials and the means by which Holmes thought we could aid him and of course, being Lyme, we also discussed the recent appearances of the alleged ghost of Mary Anning which had set the town alight with talk. If one could believe in spectres anywhere, then that place would be Lyme Regis where history walks its streets in an almost tangible manner.

I had hoped to walk up to my old friend, Dr Godfrey Jacob's house before the hour Sherlock Holmes was due to meet with us, but it proved to be impossible as our leisurely talk over breakfast extended that meal to almost ten o' clock which was when we were expecting Holmes.

Punctual in a way I had rarely known, he duly arrived at the appointed time with a sheaf of papers under his arm. With him were Sergeant Joseph Street and young Legg.

"Paolo Campini, Meredith Eccles, Giorge Marantz, Jacob Lowenstein, Sebastian Morland," he announced to a thoroughly, for the most part, bewildered audience, who were seated around the dining-table. "I pay a good deal of attention to matters of detail as you all may have observed and these papers here contain all the information I have gathered on the men I have just named with additional facts supplied by my brother who is as well versed in these matters as I am myself."

"And who are these men, Mr Holmes?" asked Street.

"Agents who steal secrets and sell them to the highest bidder".

"Any one of these men may be in Lyme hoping to do a little business at the expense of the Admiralty," I stated.

"Succinctly put, Watson." Holmes said.

"Thank you, Holmes."

"I have photographs, descriptions; known aliases and any little idiosyncrasies that they may exhibit from time to time. Watson likens this search to the proverbial search for a needle in a haystack and a needle that we cannot be sure is even present at that. Add to this list the names of Charles Leclerc and Hans Sulzbach and we have quite a line up."

"What is it that any of these men may want to steal, Mr Holmes?" asked Street.

"According to the top brass of the Royal Navy it is the plans for the new submarine and its attendant weaponry, which is being trialled offshore here. I harbour doubts, that great though the prize may be, that any of these men would display the necessary resourcefulness to attempt to steal such plans from under the noses of the Admiralty," Holmes said, "Yet it will do no harm to be vigilant."

I interjected. "The Admiralty also appear to have the notion that agents acting for foreign powers or those foreign powers themselves may attempt to make away with the vessel itself."

"It does not appear to me to be very likely," said Street.

"Nevertheless, we must allow for every contingency, it has long been an axiom of mine, although I fear even I would be powerless to prevent such a theft."

"What you are proposing then is that we all should be on the lookout for any of these men and presumably any other suspicious behaviour?" asked Beatrice sweetly.

"Yes Mrs Watson, I wish I could be more definite in what we are to look out for, but we will have to rely on our instincts."

"John," Beatrice said, to me with a smile, "Please let's holiday in Lyme by ourselves next time. Mr Holmes seems to embroil us in the wildest of schemes."

"Not all of his own making though. He is a victim of circumstances as much as we are," I said, interceding on Holmes's behalf.

"No, John, Mr Holmes may be a victim of circumstances, but *we* are victims of Mr Holmes!"

All this time Constable Legg had been looking most distracted, perhaps understandingly so and at last he spoke up.

"Instead of this talk of spies and agents, can we not just find out who threatened me last night? Especially as you, Mr Holmes, seem to take the view it was no mere joke. Sorry, sarge, but it fair rankles with me."

"Don't worry, John," said Street, "it would make my blood boil too. Do you see any kind of connection between these notes and your own particular mission here, Mr Holmes?"

"None presents itself to my mind, Sergeant," replied Holmes.

"At least the violence was contained to the breaking of a window rather than a physical attack on you both. After all, it would have been just as simple an act to throw a form of incendiary device through the two windows," Street said.

"Perhaps our mystery man is satisfied with their handiwork and this is the last we will hear from them," I ventured.

"I don't think you can rely on that, John. If he has a specific grudge against Mr Holmes or Constable Legg than he may have not been willing to put other's lives at risk," commented Beatrice.

"I admit that may be the case in the incident which happened here yet it was not the case at Legg's house for he was alone."

"Indeed so, Watson," said Holmes, "but the fact that Mrs Legg was away may have been unknown to our stone-throwing friend."

For my part, I could not fathom why Legg and Holmes had been singled out in this manner. They had met just briefly over the last five years and probably only exchanged a handful of words from what I could recall. There was nothing to my mind which bound them together yet someone obviously thought so. If a resident of the town than surely he has had ample opportunities in the past to take the action he had recently taken. Although the last investigation that Sherlock Holmes undertook in the town was in 1898 he had visited the town a few times since then. Why now, was my thought? Why now?

"A very good question, Watson," said Holmes, breaking in on my thoughts.

I was no longer surprised at this feat of Holmes's, to read my innermost thoughts for I knew that my every thought and notion was etched in my features and transparent to the man. I had endeavoured to apply this same technique with my patients, with variable degrees of success it has to be said!

"Perhaps our time would be better spent looking for this individual than chasing after spies and the like," I suggested.

"An even smaller needle in this haystack of yours, Watson. It would be a fruitless task with almost no data to work with."

With that we returned once more to the problems of the Admiralty. Holmes informed us that the plans would be kept in a safe at the Royal Lion on the floor above the Admiralty suite and guarded day and night. There were separate sections for the submarine itself, its propulsion system and its weaponry. The whole amounted to well over one hundred and fifty pages. The guard detail would be commanded by Lieutenant Webb which did not instil very much confidence to my mind, but obviously his superior officers knew better, hopefully.

"Is everything to do with the submarine to be tested then, Mr Holmes?" asked Nathaniel.

"Yes indeed, Nathaniel. Its ability to manoeuvre on the surface and below, its speed and how its weapons can be discharged and of course their effectiveness."

"How will they test the weapons? And what are they?" asked Elizabeth.

"The submarine uses both depth charges and torpedoes. As I understand it, the new depth charges detonate at a much greater depth than has been possible before and in line with this, the torpedoes are faster, more streamlined and less likely to veer off course than previous models. One of the wrecks which litter the bay will be the target for the depth charges which will be dropped while the submarine is on the surface. It is an old coal carrying vessel, the 'Franciska' which sank in the early days of December 1889. A target of perhaps below medium, size, being only two hundred and five feet in length and laying some fifty yards below the surface. One of the ships belonging to the Navy's flotilla will tow a suitable target into the area to test the torpedoes' appetite for destruction."

"How is the submarine launched, from the harbour?" asked Nathaniel.

"No, from one of the destroyers, a specially designed one I believe," Holmes replied.

"Surely then, the Admiralty's fears that the submarine itself may be stolen away must be just so much nonsense for how could anyone even think of such an action let alone get away with it," I said.

"You may have a point, Watson, the fears seem groundless to me also, but as we have said so many times before, we must allow for every eventuality."

A knocking at the door just then interrupted our flow and just as the knock sounded officious so too was our visitor, Lieutenant Matthew Webb.

"Good morning, sir," he said, addressing Holmes, "I am instructed to take you to the committee, who are assembled on the Cobb to watch the launch of the new submarine. Not that it's an order, well it was an order given to me, but it's a request they make of you, not an order. Hope that's clear sir?"

"Yes, thank you, Lieutenant. As clear as it can be. I am all but finished here so I will indeed accompany you."

We declined Holmes's invitation to go along with him for this event as we all had plans to fulfil for our time today notwithstanding Holmes's mission for us. Beatrice was very sweet in that she said she did not mind if I wanted to observe the launch, but even though it would have been of undoubted interest, discretion being the part of valour, I opted to remain with my family.

Nathaniel had some spring gardening to attend to for a local family to help earn his crust as all fishing in the bay had been suspended for the duration of the trials. Beatrice, Elizabeth and I were paying a visit to Mrs Irene Hannington, who had not only become a very close friend of Beatrice's, but was also Elizabeth's aunt. Mrs Hannington lived just to the north of Lyme, just off the road to Axminster, in a house which had wonderful views across the town and out to sea.

Sergeant Street and Constable Legg had their duties to attend to and just as they were set to leave, Belinda, Street's wife, appeared with a message that had been given to her by a young girl. The gist of this message was that there had been a break-in at the home of Henry Matravers, a local artist and could either the Sergeant or Constable attend.

"Odd," said Street, "I wonder who the message has come from for surely Henry is still in Rye at his sister's home."

"The message was given to me by young Josey Farmer who said it came to her from an elderly gentleman who approached her in Colway Lane," said Belinda.

"I'll go, Sarge, Henry's housekeeper may have looked in during his absence and discovered the break-in and rather than leaving the house has enlisted the aid of another to get word to us."

"Off you go then, John and report to me when you get back please."

Within a few minutes the previously full house had emptied and we all went our separate ways. They sky was overcast and the threat of rain was ever present as we made our way up the river towards Mrs Hannington's. The river walk was both scenic and peaceful and was yet another one of those delights than Lyme provides in abundance. The thought of retiring here was always foremost in my mind, but alas I feared that particular state was some way off yet.

Lyme encouraged dreamers and I fell squarely into that category. It was now seven years after my first visit and the pull and allure of the place remained as strong as ever. The strangest feeling was not that I belonged to this town, but rather that the town somehow belonged to me.

58

The Royal Navy trials in the bay have got underway with the minimum of fuss and nothing by way of fanfare. Officialdom was the order of the day as the top brass of the Admiralty gathered on the end of the Cobb to witness the launch of a new class of submarine. It is to be hoped that the trials will be over with quickly to enable the fishermen of the town to go about their business. This view is not un-patriotic, but realistic, for our own men of the sea have families to feed too.

There have been further 'sightings' of Mary Anning's ghost in many parts of the town. We make no further comment on this, the views of this newspaper on the subject are well known to you all.

A reminder that time is running out to vote for the best dressed shop window in town. Get those votes in!

Chapter Seven

After spending a most agreeable afternoon with Mrs Hannington we wandered back down into Lyme, refreshed and happy. Nathaniel was evidently still busy with his gardening and we settled down in the parlour with cups of tea all round. Hardly had we done so when there came yet another knock at the door, it must be the most knocked door in Lyme I idly thought. This time it was Sergeant Street in the doorway.

"Hullo, Doctor, Mrs Watson, Elizabeth. Have you come across young John on your travels? I was called away myself and have only just realised that he has not returned from Mr Matravers's house."

"He may have picked up a lead and gone to follow it up," I replied.

"Possibly so, but all the same I will wander up there and take a look, I don't suppose you would care for a further walk, Doctor Watson?"

It was the last thing I cared to do quite honestly, but Beatrice and Elizabeth both urged me to lend my assistance so I felt somewhat compelled to offer my services in whatever capacity Street thought I may be of use in.

Henry Matravers occupied a house near Sleech woods; even though it was only a few minutes' walk out of Lyme it seemed much more remote and isolated because of its location. The house itself looked somehow as though austerity had come knocking one dark day and been invited to stay, but perhaps artists preferred their dwellings this way, both rustic and Bohemian.

We could see no sign of life as we approached the tumble-down house, but we heard what sounded like a faint cry. The house was locked and the stout doors showed every sign of resisting whatever pressure we would apply to them. The sound came to our ears once more and this time we able to pin point where it was coming from; the rear of the house. On entering what passed for a rear garden, although it had more the appearance of a wilderness, we at once saw the prostrate form of Legg in the rear porch. The blood had collected underneath him forming a pool of crimson. We turned him to his side carefully and he let out another slight noise akin to a whimper. That he had been stabbed now became obvious and the direction and purpose of the thrust told to us of how it was meant to enter his heart, only Legg's pocket-book had saved him, deflecting the knife away from its intended target. The flow of blood had slowed already, but I was able to staunch it completely within a few seconds. Legg displayed other injuries, some no doubt as a result of trying to ward off what would have been a fatal blow were it not for his pocket-book, indeed could still prove to be fatal unless the necessary steps were taken. The chief difficulty before us was the task of getting Legg to a place of safety, the terrain and narrow path that led to Matraver's house would make it no easy task for stretcher bearers to effect the recovery of Legg.

Sergeant Street struck out for Lyme whilst I remained with the young constable, giving him such help and succour as I could. I also availed myself of the opportunity to survey the scene closely in the manner of Holmes himself. I gathered up a few cigarette ends which lay in the vicinity of the porch, that they were fresh was not in doubt and the likelihood is that they had been smoked by the unknown perpetrator as he waited for Legg to become ensnared in his trap, for it seemed obvious to me that the whole tale of a break-in was a fabrication. I placed the cigarette ends into my pocket knowing that Holmes would wish to study them and I had no doubts at all that he would be able to obtain a wealth of information from this seemingly smallest of clues. Legg's pulse although weak was steady and gave me some idea of the man's fight to survive. An hour must have gone by before I could hear the sound of voices coming towards me. Street duly came into view and along with him three men who I did not recognise, but were introduced to me as three members of the fishing community who were temporarily idle whilst the Navy did its testing and trials. They bore with them a temporary stretcher which looked

61

rather like the pared-down hull of a boat which is exactly what it turned out to be. These three burly men belied their strength as they laid Legg down on this makeshift transport with a gentleness I would scarcely have credited them with.

"Hold on, John," whispered Street, "stay with us, you are going to come through this."

Legg was carried sure footedly in spite of the narrow paths and undulating field we had to negotiate before coming back to a recognised pathway. It had been decided by Street to take the constable to Dr Jacobs's very well equipped surgery and then make our plans once we had ascertained the full nature of his wounds. My companions bore their load stoically with no word of complaint passing their lips at any stage of the journey. The spirit of the town became apparent to me once more for as we approached Lyme the path became thronged with well-wishers, who having heard of the attack, came to lend their support to Legg.

"Hang in there Johnny."
"You will be fine."
"We'll get whoever did this to you."

They were just some of these voices that carried to me and there was certainly no shortage of volunteers to help in carrying the stricken man. When we arrived at Dr Jacobs's practice Legg was carried in very gingerly and laid down on the bed in the surgery. The examination could now start in earnest. We cleaned the wounds that we could see and checked for other injuries, thankfully there were none, other than slight scratches. The injuries though severe in themselves were not life-threatening in our opinion; that is not to say that we not aware of the seriousness of the injuries inflicted, but we were confident that we could pull him through. I worked quickly to cleanse and close the knife wound and remarked to Jacobs just how lucky Legg had been. His breathing was returning to normal and he responded to our voices although he could not speak himself yet.

The good sergeant had gone to seek out young Josey and to make a report of the incident which would be forwarded to the police station at Bridport. A small crowd had gathered outside Jacob's home in Monmouth Street, hoping for news. There was a frenzied knocking at the door and Jacob's wife, Sarah ushered in a young lady who had an abject look of terror on her face.

"I tried to stop her, Godfrey," said Sarah.

"Don't worry Sarah, she has every right to be here," replied Jacobs.

"My poor John," she cried. She then noticed the blood soaked clothing on the floor and began to sway, but I caught her before she fainted dead away.

"It's worse than it looks, he is doing very well. I am Dr John Watson; it was I who found him along with Sergeant Street.

"I am John's intended; Elizabeth Markey, but I much prefer the shorter version of my name."

"Very well. Pleased to meet you, Eliza."

"No, I meant I prefer to be called Beth," she said.

"Apologies, please do not worry, Beth, he is in the most capable of hands, those of Dr Jacobs here. John is a fit, young man and will come through this."

"What injuries has he?"

"A blow to the head and a knife wound which fortunately missed its intended target, the heart."

Whilst I was replying to Beth, Jacobs had hastily pulled up a sheet around Legg's chest.

"Who did this thing?" she cried, "John has no enemies in the town."

"At this stage, we have precious little to go on, but my friend, Mr Sherlock Homes, whom you may have heard of, is here in Lyme and if anyone can get to the bottom of this, then it is he."

"I have heard of him yes. John told me how he reminded him of my father, not that I have ever met him, Sherlock Holmes of course I mean, I have met my father frequently," she exclaimed with a nervous laugh which masked her very real concern.

I asked her whether John had confided in her regarding the episode of the stone-throwing and its apparent threatening note. She replied in the affirmative, but like the constable himself, she was completely in the dark as to who could be behind such a thing. As well as my concern for our patient, my thoughts were also of Holmes for he too had been a recipient of a threat and I had no need of Holmes's deductive powers to realise that just as the unfortunate policeman had been, so Holmes himself could be a victim of this unknown assailant.

We allowed young Beth to sit with Legg for a while before we resumed our treatment. Once the swelling attendant with each wound had subsided then we could make good our efforts to doctor the injuries he had sustained. She held his hand and comforted him with loving talk of the future they would enjoy together. I reasoned to Jacobs that not only had we to aid Legg's recovery, but also to try to afford him a degree of protection for whoever attacked him was still at large and once he realised his murderous onslaught had failed he may well have plans to finish the job he had started as well as dealing with Sherlock Holmes. Sergeant Street returned, having made his report and was full of concern for his younger colleague who had also become a good friend over the few years they had worked together. He informed us that a inspector would be sent out from Bridport as soon as was possible in the guise of an Inspector Baker who we hoped was more enlightened than his predecessor, Inspector Baddeley, who was somewhat insufferable and had been determined not to enlist the aid of Holmes in our previous investigations here. Street excused himself for he still had his other duties to perform and Jacobs and I our medical duties to resume.

The people of Lyme are aghast at the news that our very own constable, John Legg, has been the subject of a vicious attack by person or persons unknown. The attack took place at the home of local artist, Henry Matravers. We should stress that Mr Matravers is not a suspect, being away in deepest Sussex at the moment. I am sure you will all join with us in praying for John's speedy recovery and if anyone has any information that may help in bringing his assailant to book then please contact Sergeant Joe Street at the police house.

There has been a call to create a special path along the seafront for exclusive use of those who wish to ride their bicycles and penny-farthings. We are not in favour of this plan believing that paths along the seafront should remain for pedestrians only and those who care to bicycle can leave their contraptions in a secure place and join the rest of Lyme in promenading along the 'Walk' using feet not pedals!

Chapter Eight

The news of the attack on John Legg which had filtered down the whole length and breadth of the town had obviously now come to the attention of Holmes for he arrived at Jacobs's Monmouth Street house and surgery just some twenty minutes after Miss Beth Markey's arrival. He neither disturbed Miss Markey's vigil nor examined Legg, but took me to one side in order to listen to my account of how we found the constable.

Succinctly as I could I apprised Holmes of the afternoon's events leading up to the discovery of the unfortunate man and the nature of his injuries.

"Have you questioned him as regards the attack?"

"He is no state to be questioned nor will he be for some while yet I fear. Sergeant Street has asked Josey Farmer what she remembers about the man who gave her the message, but to no avail, she barely seems to have noticed him at all. I did find these at the scene of the crime," I said, and handed Holmes the cigarette ends I had gathered up.

Holmes took these over to the light and examined them closely, pausing only to bring each one to his hawk-like nose. Satisfied with whatever these remnants had told him, he promptly threw them on the floor. I duly picked them up not wishing to incur the wrath of Sarah Jacobs who I reckoned would not take to kindly to having her floor used as some kind of receptacle for the detritus of Holmes's evidence. I knew Holmes had made a special study of cigar ash, tobacco and cigarettes, indeed he had written a monograph upon the subject so I was tolerably sure that these fragments had yielded something of their origin to his trained eye.

"What do they tell you?"

"The brand of cigarette is one that goes by the name of, '*Wincanton*' for it was in that town that it originated. The banding and flavour is quite distinct. Its distribution is not nationwide however and tends to be confined to an area spanning the east of Devon, through Dorset to Wiltshire. It is perhaps an acquired taste rather like the area's cider!"

"Can you deduce anything regarding the smoker?"

"If I was truly a wizard that your readers may imagine me to be after devouring your embellished tales all these years, then I would no doubt be able to furnish you with the man's age, his height, his weight, his shoe size and more importantly, his whereabouts. Alas, I can do none of those things except tell you that he uses 'Parisienne' cologne which is hardly a surprise to either one of us."

Holmes swept into the surgery proper and with a cursory glance at Miss Markey, he proceeded to spread out Legg's clothes on the floor and ran his fingers through the pockets and folds of his uniform.

"What have we here?" he cried to himself as he withdrew a slip of paper which had been in the inner pocket of Legg's jacket.

"Why don't you bring it into the hallway?" I asked as casually as I could, motioning Holmes to look at the stricken face of young Beth.

"What? Oh yes, of course."

The message we read on this piece of paper was stark and uncompromising for it said: John Legg-Killer no more.

"A very thorough man this would be killer of ours. This note was prepared some time before the event, note the creases which are hardly fresh, but indicative of having been carried around for some little time, perhaps being transferred between garments."

"What worries me, Holmes is that this man will seek to finish off what he has started with regard to Legg," I said, in a whisper, not wishing my words to carry to the surgery, "and further, that this man is carrying around with him a similar note bearing your name."

"Your worries are well founded, Watson. We must take steps to protect Constable Legg and keep him safe from further harm."

"That protection can only take place here for I do not propose he be moved for some little time yet."

"Very well, can he be moved safely to a room at the rear of the house? I believe there is such a room in that area with no outside access, if I recall correctly."

"I see no reason why not and yes you do recall correctly, but before we go any further with our plans, we should be inviting the views of Dr Jacobs and his family, after all this is their home and their safety is paramount too."

We went through to the family quarters where we found Godfrey, Sarah and the children, Arthur, Cecil and Violet who had just returned home from their respective schools. Arthur and Cecil were now fast approaching becoming young men and were as sturdily built as their father with whom I had played rugby for Blackheath many, many years ago. Violet was now seven years old and as delightful as ever.

Holmes detailed the situation to them and pulled no punches when outlining how Legg could be subject to another attack which may imperil the whole household. The Jacobs family stood firm and left us in no uncertain terms that Legg was under their protection from now on.

A spare room, formerly the nursery, was made ready for its new incumbent and it was agreed to move Legg that evening. We had no doubts that we could devise a rota whereby he would not be left unattended at any time of the day or night.

"I will go and tell Miss Markey that we need to move him, without telling her the reasons for so doing," I said.

Young Beth looked scarcely to have moved; she was still holding Legg's left hand tightly and still talking to him in a soft whisper. His eyelids were fluttering and although he had not yet recovered the powers of communication, I believed he heard and understood every word. I explained to her that we needed to move him to a more comfortable bed and to render the surgery free for the doctor's patients the following morning.

"Will I be able to come back later?" she entreated.

"Yes of course, Beth. Why don't you give us an hour to put the arrangements into force and come back then?"

"Thank you, Doctor and thank you for finding and saving him."

She passed Sergeant Street in the hall as she exited and he entered. He laid a kindly hand upon her shoulder and whispered in her ear, words of encouragement and comfort too no doubt. We outlined to Street the measures we were taking and he seemed satisfied with those steps.

"I will spend the night here, if that is acceptable to you and your family, Doctor Jacobs?" Street announced.

"Perfectly so," replied Jacobs, "as long as it is all right with Belinda, Joe!"

"It will be, she is as concerned as I am, John is like family. Tell me though, Mr Holmes, who protects you?"

"I assure you, Sergeant that I would not have survived as long as I did in my chosen profession without knowing a thing or two about protecting myself. For instance, I have some knowledge of baritsu, or the Japanese style of wrestling, which has more than once been very useful to me. Besides, I have no doubts that Watson will be good enough to offer me the use of his old service revolver which I am confident he packed along with his spare collars."

Together, Jacobs, Street and I shifted John Legg to his temporary new quarters. I was pleased to see how the swelling had subsided around the area of his injuries. I was able to cleanse the knife wound once more whilst marvelling again just how fortunate he had been. I had hopes that by the morning he may be recovered enough to give an account of what had befallen him and who his assailant was. Holmes and I left the constable to his new charges and walked back to Coombe Street.

"Are you joining us for an evening meal, Holmes or does the Admiralty have call on you tonight?"

"If I am welcome, then yes, I will spend the evening with you."

"It goes without saying that you are welcome. What news from the launch of the submarine?"

"All went well as far as I could ascertain. The finest binoculars in the world would only be useful up to the point where the vessel disappeared beneath the waves. I lost a certain amount of interest after that despite the best efforts of various Navy officials who sought to engage me with tales of the submarine's alleged prowess.

They were at great pains to point out to me how naval warfare becomes impossible within the radius of an *A-class* submarine. When I pointed out to them that much the same was said about the *Bruce-Partington* submarine, then they tried to persuade me no more!"

"So, no sign of agents or spies on the horizon then?"

"None whatsoever, the more I consider it the more I am inclined to the view that I have been assigned a wild-goose chase either by design or by accident I do not know."

"Are you saying then, that in spite of the Admiralty seeking your assistance through Mycroft, their fears are unfounded and they know so?"

"I do not rule that out, Watson."

"If that should prove to be the case then why all this rigmarole of having you here? It makes no sense to me."

"We may yet see light where there is no light presently," Homes replied laconically.

"You do seem particularly bothered, Holmes I have to say."

"What will be, will be, Watson, but I have to say that retirement seems to be a particularly busy state for me. Not only do I find myself embroiled in God knows what here, but my services are requested by all and sundry to investigate perceived miscarriages of justice and what have you."

"Do any of these requests interest you to any great extent?"

"Some have points of interest, others I would not waste my precious time on. The latest entreaty for help has come from the family of Mrs Jane Cox."

"I am not familiar with the name."

"There is no reason why you should be unless you are a student of crime. She was a witness who testified at the inquest into the death by poisoning of the young barrister, Charles Bravo in 1876. Her family believe that she was hard done by and was left with suspicion attached to her that she had not been entirely honest in her testimony."

"The case does ring a bell with me, was not Bravo's wife acquitted of his murder?"

"No, Watson, for the simple reason there was no trial, just two inquests."

"And is there any foundation to her family's grievances?"

"Well, yes, but not quite in the way that they believe for it is obvious to me that Jane Cox did indeed lie under oath at the inquests and for perhaps, the best possible reason."

"Which was?"

"She was guilty of the crime herself, there can be no doubt of that."

"Will you communicate this to her family?"

"I think not, Watson. I will let sleeping dogs lie and politely turn down their request."

By this time we had reached Nathaniel and Elizabeth's cottage and as I stepped into the hall I was accosted by a shaggy mass which hurtled out of nowhere like an errant cannonball.

"Isn't she an angel, Uncle John?" shrilled Elizabeth.

I must admit it was not a view I felt I could subscribe to wholly. To my mind the dog displayed far too healthy an interest in my boots and trouser turn-ups to warrant an epithet of 'angel'.

"Where has she appeared from?" I asked, trying to keep any note of displeasure out of my voice.

"The family Nathaniel was working for today, on their garden, you know, gave him this lovely angelic creature," she replied, far too excitedly in my opinion. "We have named her Angel!"

"They just handed the dog over? Perhaps they had a good reason for doing so. She may be overly aggressive for instance. Any more of her attentions and I will be needing a new pair of boots!"

"Sorry, Uncle John," and with that she dragged the beast away.

"I see you have been making the acquaintance of Angel, John," laughed Beatrice as I entered the parlour.

"Somehow I sense she may struggle to live up to her name, she is somewhat perky if not downright mischievous."

"She will settle down and become part of the family," Nathaniel said.

I harrumphed as loudly as I could under the circumstances which had already dictated I was to be the villain of the day. I have never looked kindly on another dog since being forced to part with my bull-pup some twenty-two years ago.

Holmes and I sat down and filled our pipes in comparative peace as we brought everybody up to date on all the events of the day and the state of John Legg's health. The whole house, including Angel fortunately, was silenced by the enormity of what could have happened. Instead of sitting comfortably discussing Legg's recovery, we could well have been mourning his loss. We busied ourselves with laying the table for the evening meal and an unusually sombre affair it promised to be. Just as we declared ourselves ready to eat, there was a knock at the door, as I was closest to the hall I went to open the door.

"Ah, Lydia!"

"Doctor Watson! Hullo."

Although as far as we can ascertain there has been no progress in arresting anyone for the assault on John Legg, we are pleased to have received news of his continuing recovery from the injuries he sustained. It may be noted that the celebrated detective, Mr Sherlock Holmes is in Lyme at present and it is to be hoped that police will look to him for aid in solving this heinous crime.

It has been announced that the next show at the Victoria Hall is to be a musical celebration of the world of nursery rhymes. This will be brought to us by the well known impresarios, Harold Long and Timothy Bell.

With the closure of Miss Lydia Hutching's show it is to be hoped there will be no more talk of ghosts and phantoms abroad in the town.

Chapter Nine

"Look who we have here, come to see us," I proudly announced.

"I'm sorry," Lydia said, "I am disturbing your meal."

"Nonsense, Lydia," Beatrice said, "Have you eaten? If not, pull up a chair and join us. If you have eaten, pull up a chair and join us anyway!"

Lydia did so and we all engaged in a slight re-distribution of the food on our plates, to enable her to have a portion approximately equal to all of us although I rapidly came to the conclusion that rather more had left my plate than anybody else's!

Lydia was extremely garrulous on subject of her one woman show, understandably so for it was an undeniable reason for feeling proud. The show had become a great success, the first of many I felt for this talented young woman.

"There are just the two more shows left and they are both sold out completely, there will not even be standing room."

"That's wonderful, Lydia," I enthused warmly, "but it will mean that we will not be able to see the show for ourselves and I was looking forward very much to seeing it, as we all were."

"Sorry, Doctor Watson, I had not thought of that."

"You are a victim of your own success, young lady," said Holmes and I caught the merest tone of chastisement in his tone. "Perhaps you should split whatever monies you earn with the ghost of Mary Anning."

Lydia shifted somewhat nervously in her seat and picked at her food absent-mindedly. "I am glad to say it has not affected sales adversely."

"No, indeed, rather the reverse. Fortunate don't you think or do you have no views on that aspect of the matter?" Holmes asked.

"Really, Holmes," I remonstrated, "Lydia has come to see us to share her good news and friendship with us, not to be interrogated over matters she has no control over."

Holmes nodded curtly, but with no word of apology and the conversation passed on to other subjects, subjects as diverse as bees, photography, the American Civil War, the works of Charles Dickens and the history of coal production.

After we had finished eating and the dishes had been cleared away we were all able to relax with the exception of Lydia who had a show to do that evening.

"Where did you get the idea for the show, Lydia?" asked Beatrice.

"Oh, it just came to me while I was watching a similar sort of show in London. It was a one man production on the life of Sir Francis Drake told through rhyme, words and song. I thought, 'I could do that!' and started mapping the show out that very evening."

"Did you gain work that was plentiful enough for you during your time in London?" I asked.

"Yes, I was very fortunate and managed to get work in the legitimate theatres so to speak and also in the music halls doing monologues and recitals. Hard work, but enormously good for my stagecraft. I worked with a very famous quick-change artist who taught me the tricks of his trade which have come in very handy in my show."

"Leonardo Fregoli?" asked Holmes.

"Yes, the best in the world," she replied.

"So I believe," rejoined Holmes, displaying a hitherto unknown knowledge of the varieties.

"If you like, because you are likely to miss the show, I can give you an idea of how it all works here and now. Obviously there will be lots I have to take out and there are no props or changes of costume so you will have to rely on your imagination."

"Thank you Lydia, that would be just perfect," I said.

We moved the table and chairs to one side of the room and tried to create as much space as we could for Lydia's impromptu performance. We gathered ourselves together in a semi-circle and Lydia was centre stage and ready to begin.

"*I am well known throughout the whole of Europe,*" she announced and proceeded to take us on a magical journey through the life of Mary Anning. Characters from all walks of life came to life, scientists for instance such as, Henry De La Beche, William Buckland, Louis Agassiz and even King Frederick Augustus III of Saxony. Each of these was played to perfection by Lydia who inhabited each of these individuals and became them. We had the story of Mary's life from when she was born in poverty until when she died, also in poverty. All the highs and lows were there, the discoveries, the friendship with the Philpot sisters of Lyme, the deaths of her father and mother and her beloved dog, Tray.

We laughed and we cried at the magic that Lydia was displaying, at the emotions that she brought to the surface so ably. Her facial expressions and her physical dexterity were a joy to behold. All this was in the name of entertainment, but even so Lydia opened up Mary Anning's life for all to see and wonder at and gave a great insight into an exceptional person's life.

"*Ladies and gentlemen, the celebrated Mary Anning.*" With that, the celebrated Miss Lydia Hutchings concluded her mesmerising performance. We stood as one and applauded. Lydia curtsied with a flourish and prepared to take her leave for another performance was due before the evening's paying customers. As she said her goodbyes and walked into the hall, I heard Sherlock Holmes say, softly to her as she passed him.

"It has to stop, Lydia, it really must."

Lydia locked her brown eyes on to Holmes's unblinking grey ones. There followed an almost imperceptible nod.

"You are right. Consider it stopped, Mr Holmes."

"Thank you, Lydia."

There was no time to question Holmes about this exchange for as Lydia left the house, Joe Street entered it.

"Good evening, folks, I am the bearer of glad tidings, John is fully conscious and talking. I haven't questioned him about the attack, not while Beth was with him, but I have sent her home now and I thought you, Mr Holmes, may wish to question him."

"By all means, Sergeant as long as our twin medicos grant me their permission to do so."

"That is easily decided, Holmes, I will come back up to Jacobs's with you, if Beatrice has no objections."

"No of course not John, but please try not to be late, I am sure the Royal Lion can manage without your custom for one evening!"

My boots had become once more a source of great entertainment for Angel whose mouth and teeth seemed to become highly excited in my presence. As much as I was pleased to see she displayed a fine set of molars I was not overly keen that she test them on any part of my attire or indeed me.

"Uncle John," said Elizabeth, "perhaps you would care to take Angel for a walk at the same time, as you are going out anyway?"

"I fear not, Elizabeth, the responsibility would be too great. What if I were to lose her?"

"Well, honestly now, is that likely?" retorted Elizabeth.

"I assure you, not only is it likely, but entirely probable!"

I made my escape in the company of Holmes and Street for the very short walk to Jacobs's house in Monmouth Street. I fervently wished that John Legg would be able to tell us who had assaulted him and armed with that information we could set about apprehending him.

Constable Legg certainly looked a lot brighter and indeed healthier than he had just a few hours previously. Colour had returned to his cheeks and he was able to give us a smile of welcome.

"I have always said that Lyme is an exciting place to be, but maybe this is stretching things too far," he joked.

"What of the incident, can you recall anything about your attacker?" asked Holmes.

"Very little, Mr Holmes. I remember clearly approaching the rear porch, but the events after that are a bit of a blur I'm afraid. I did get the impression that the man, if it was a man, that attacked me was tall, I recall a shadow leaning over me which gave me that impression."

"Anything else you recall could be useful; the merest intimation would be uniformly helpful."

"No, there is nothing other than feeling a blow on the head and from then on I did not feel anything at all. I just found myself in a world of dreams, weird, fractured and vivid. Wait, though, I seem to recall a strange, overpowering scent, does that sound odd?"

"No, not at all for we know that our man favours 'Parisienne' cologne, strongly so in fact, perhaps it may serve to camouflage a distinctive body odour," Holmes replied.

"What is our next step?" asked Legg.

"Your next step is simple," I interjected, "all you have to do is rest and do as the doctor orders."

"That is exactly what Beth said to me the very moment I opened my eyes."

"Unless you want to feel the wrath of Miss Markey, Dr Jacobs and me, then that is precisely what you will do!"

"And that's a direct order from your sergeant too," added Street.

"Yes sir!" and he sank back further onto the pillow. We left the man to his sleep and prescribed rest.

"We appear to be no further forward, Holmes," I ventured.

"We do have the information now that we didn't have before, that our man is tall," Holmes replied.

"I must admit, I cannot see how this is information that we can act on and remember it was only Legg's impression."

"I concede to you that it not the most singular clue we could have uncovered, but it is a clue all the same. What news from Inspector Baker, Sergeant?"

"I expect we will see him in the morning, Mr Holmes."

"Excellent, we will confer tomorrow then if I am not murdered in my bed!"

"You will be safe, Holmes, you have the navy there to protect you and I believe the Royal Lion management decided long ago that guests being murdered in their beds was somewhat of a hindrance to their continued success," I said, drily, "and if that is not comfort enough then please allow me to escort you to the hotel once more."

"Thank you, Watson, but please do not fall foul of Mrs Watson by so doing. At my time of life I do not desire to be a material witness in the divorce courts!"

"Very droll, Holmes."

Prayers have been said at St Michaels Church for the continuing recovery of John Legg. Inspector Baker from Bridport has arrived to take over the investigation. Our advice to the inspector is to seek out Sherlock Holmes at the earliest opportunity. Sergeant Street has called for calm and vigilance.

There have been yet more calls for the creation of a children's boat pond. This is another thorny problem which seems to vex our town council with some councillors even debating the need for such a facility and questioning why children should be favoured this way. Our view is that it is a very fine idea and the council should stop dragging its heels and provide this boat pond before the fashion for such activities is replaced by something else.

'The Trials Of Mary Anning' has now ended its run and we take this opportunity to wish Miss Lydia Hutchings continued success in her career, but....come back soon, Lydia!

Chapter Ten

We could hear the sound of laughter and merriment coming from the Lounge bar of the Royal Lion before we entered its portal. The interior was unusually bright and welcoming and my resolve began to weaken before we had hardly crossed the threshold.

"Do you have to report to the Naval Secrets Committee?" I asked.

"If I do, it would be a fleeting appearance before them, for I have nothing of any consequence to report. In fact, I have nothing inconsequential either!"

"Perhaps it is for the best with this other business hanging over you like a Damoclean sword."

"Good old Watson, as direct and to the point as always."

"I swear sometimes, that you have as little regard for your own personal safety then is healthy for you!"

"It is stupidity rather than courage to refuse to recognise danger when it is close upon you and upon my word, Watson, you know me not to be stupid, but as yet we have only the vaguest idea how this danger will spring and in what shape or form so for now a warming brandy will hit the mark rather than ceaseless worrying."

We ordered our drinks at the bar and retired to the corner seats we had occupied the previous evening. There were a few familiar faces in the bar and we exchanged nods of greeting and pleasantries with four or five folk. Lyme being such a small town, it was impossible not to stumble across people known to you wherever you went. It is I think, one of the town's more endearing qualities.

"I hope the peace will not be shattered tonight by spectres and ghosts, Holmes."

"I can tell you for certain that the ghost of Mary Anning has been laid to rest and will walk no more."

"Have you now taken to communing with spirits, Holmes?"

"Mary Anning, as seen by the good people of Lyme, was rather more earthbound than they imagined."

"Lydia!!" I exclaimed, spilling my brandy in the process.

"Ah, Watson, the penny has dropped. Yes, Lydia was responsible for the sightings in a novel, but altogether misguided way to drum up more business for her show."

"Hence your word to her as she left Nathaniel's tonight."

"Indeed."

"Did she confess beforehand?"

"No, but there was no pressing need for her to do so. She knew that I knew and that was enough for both of us."

"Well, well, I would hardly have believed it of her."

"True, Watson, but at least there was no great harm done."

"That is one mystery solved at least, but we still have our mystery man watching and waiting, out there somewhere. Do you think, and it sounds outlandish as I say it, that one of the naval committee may be responsible for they are the ones who dragged you down here for what appears to be no good reason that I can fathom?"

"My dear fellow, it sounds outlandish to you because it is so. What possible reason could one of their number have for the attack on Legg?"

I felt my argument faltering beneath me like shifting sands, yet I soldiered on gamely. "It could have been a blind to throw you off your guard," I theorised.

"To the point of murdering him?" Come now, Watson, I expect better from you."

"But he was not murdered," I responded.

"Only through good fortune and a police-issue pocket-book, Watson."

It was one of those occasions when I fervently wished I had not opened my mouth. I had many memories of Holmes's words to me over the years, 'You know my methods, Watson, apply them', and of how often I was to be found lacking in both observation and conjecture. The passing years, it seemed, had not sharpened my senses. I had no time to ponder on this for when I looked up I could see the now familiar figure of Lieutenant Matthew Webb bearing down on us.

"Good evening, gentlemen. I trust you have had a good day."

"I do not believe it's one that we will look back on with any great relish, Lieutenant," I replied.

"What? Oh, anyway, Mr Holmes would you be free to report to the committee? If convenient of course."

"Tomorrow night or the night after at eight-thirty pm would be convenient to me, Lieutenant."

"Shall I say that then, sir, only I am sure they had this evening in mind, although possibly not, they did not specify."

"Come on young Webb, take me to your leaders," Holmes said, laughing and standing up, clapped Webb on the shoulder and swept him up out of the room.

Holmes had not invited me to follow him and I had not presumed to do so, but remained seated sipping my brandy. As much I wanted to return to Coombe Street and Beatrice, I thought it would be rude of me to do so in Holmes's absence and as I was not privy to how long this consultation with the Admiralty and associated officers would be, I elected to order another brandy and soda apiece for us. Resuming my seat I fell into a brown study on how so much happens in a small town like Lyme Regis. Not only our present troubles, but also those we had encountered during previous visits. Then again, throughout its long history, the town had time and time again been at the forefront of English history as a whole. If I were to liken Lyme to a boxer then it would be fair to say that the town and its people had always punched above their weight. Of our current problems I had neither answers nor much by way of a theory. The linking together of Sherlock Holmes and John Legg seemed tenuous if not downright bizarre, for the life of me I could not divine a connection between the men save for the perfunctory one of them knowing each other, albeit not very well. The time they had spent in each other's company was at best fleeting, almost to the point of non-existence, but all the same this link had been acted on with great ferocity and surely it was only a matter of time before our man would attempt to mount some kind of assault upon Holmes. Forewarned is of course forearmed and I knew better than anyone of Holmes's resourcefulness and courage in the face of danger yet a knife in the back on a dark street corner could do for anyone in spite of a certain amount of foreknowledge that such an attack may be imminent.

The reason for Holmes being here, that of looking out for spies and agents with mischief on their mind, had almost receded from my own mind. But now, when I did ponder on it, it seemed to be just as unlikely as it first sounded; with plans under lock and key guarded day and night, the submarine itself protected by a small flotilla of no doubt heavily armed ships. I could not perceive a scintilla of truth in this talk of spies, but if that was the case why was Holmes here and more pertinently, if I was on the right track with this particular theory, and I believed I was, then surely Holmes would have reasoned this out too. So, once again why was Sherlock Holmes here? Or, more to the point, why was he still here? Serving paymasters who apparently had no need of him, at least not for the reasons they had stated. I chuckled to myself, 'at least the problem of the recent spate of haunting has been solved. 'Good old Lydia!' I did not have in my heart to think of her in any other way!

My reverie was interrupted by the arrival of a youngish man, resplendent in a jacket I fear I do not have the words to describe adequately. It fell somewhere between a cloak and a mess jacket with over-sized buttons so highly polished that every light in the bar seemed to radiate out from them, I thought I would have to shield my eyes from this vision.

"I see my jacket interests you, I purchased it in Brighton," he announced, as though this fact alone would explain it away.

"I cannot recall seeing anything quite like it before," I said, quite truthfully.

"I had it specially made for me by a tailor in Hove and everywhere I went I was inundated with requests for the name of that particular tailor."

"I shouldn't wonder at it! Was that with a view to avoiding him?" I said, with a hearty laugh so as not to hurt his feelings for he seemed inordinately proud of his attire.

"It is Doctor Watson isn't it?" he enquired

"Yes it is," I said, reaching out and shaking his hand, "but you have the advantage of me."

"Matthew Johnson, you may not remember me; it was five years ago after all."

"Matthew Johnson, Matthew Johnson," I repeated, searching my memory, "of course, you were the junior clerk at Madders and Fane."

Madders and Fane were solicitors in Broad Street and in the space of a few days of madness, Robert Fane, Henry Madders, an ex-colleague James Broderick and their senior clerk, Silas Nanther were brutally murdered. This spate of killing came to an end out on the bleakness of Dartmoor with the killer meeting his end just as violently as he had treated his victims. I have my notes on the case, but I have the gravest of doubts it will ever see the light of day in a published account. Johnson was left unscathed in the midst of this violence, but ultimately found himself without employment.

"I trust you were able to find a suitable position, Mr Johnson?"

"In a manner of speaking yes, but only by moving away from the area, to Brighton in fact. Do you know the town?"

"Yes, I spent a little time there as a locum a long time ago, in the Kemp Town district. Are you here for a visit then?"

"No, I decided to move back a few months back, the pull of Lyme you know, and found employment with a local house agent."

"I am pleased for you, Mr Johnson," I said, amiably.

"It's rather an odd coincidence seeing you here and now, Doctor."

"Why so?"

"One of the properties we have put on the market this week is Silas Nanther's old place."

"I recall it. An old blacksmith's forge was it not? How many times has it changed hands during the past five years?" I asked.

"That's just it, Doctor, it hasn't. It has been standing empty since Silas's murder as we have had no instructions to sell from the current owner, Silas's brother."

"Ah yes, I recall Mr Nanther mentioning a brother who he was planning to flee to before death caught up with him."

"According to Silas's will this brother was bequeathed the house, but after the news of his brother's death and after the funeral, it seemed he had an attack of brain-fever and lapsed into what has turned out to be a temporary insanity or at least an impairment which stopped the poor man functioning for quite some time."

"And I take it he has now recovered, hence the old forge being put on the market."

"Exactly so, Doctor."

"For the life of me I cannot remember the brother's name."

"Henry," confirmed Mr Johnson.

"That's the man and where was it he was living?"

"Salisbury!" announced the the strident voice of Sherlock Holmes.

The continuing prosperity of Lyme Regis and how to take this forward into this new century was the subject of a heated debate in the town council chambers. There is no doubt the town needs to change to adapt to these modern times we now live in. The Edwardian age has ushered in with it the motor-car which will change our lives forever. Even the imminent railway link to the town will, we believe, become secondary to the motor-car. Already, the country's streets and road are changing to accommodate these machines and this is something we need to embrace here.

A collection was taken up at various inns for John Legg. As yet, there is still no arrest in connection with the assault on John.

Chapter Eleven

"Yes, Mr Holmes," said a startled Mr Johnson, "it *was* Salisbury."

"Good evening, Mr Johnson."

I started to apprise Holmes of Mr Johnson's new employ in Lyme, but it was unnecessary for Holmes had been present during the latter part of our conversation unbeknown to us.

"I'd wager Henry Nanther was the last client to call on you before you left the office," stated Holmes.

"Yes he was, although how you know this fact, I do not know."

"Elementary. The scent of 'Parisienne' cologne is detectable on your, well what shall I call it, your jacket, which if you don't mind me saying is singular in the extreme."

"Rather fetching is it not?" said Johnson, the pride in his voice apparent once more."

"I fear it is not the word I would use to describe it, Mr Johnson. Henry Nanther presumably has corresponded with you recently with regards to taking charge of his late brother's property and effects and arrived in Lyme yesterday, is that so?"

"Yes, that is so."

Holmes fished around in one of his inner pockets and brought forth the note that had been found in John Legg's jacket. He turned it over and on the reverse side of the would-be killer's gloating message was the name, *'Henry Nanther'*.

"Your handwriting I see, Holmes."

"Really, Watson, you excel yourself! Indeed, yes, I added the name to it just a short while ago while with our friends upstairs, for I found my attention had wandered somewhat. The outcome of this lapse of mindfulness on my part resulted in Henry Nanther coming forcibly into my thoughts. He, I felt, was the only link between Legg and myself that made any sense at all and Mr Johnson's words merely served as confirmation of this thought process."

"I think I see some light, Holmes."

"I am most gratified to hear it, my dear fellow."

"He blames you and Constable Legg for the death of his brother for it was you who sent Legg to watch over Silas Nanther with the dreadful results we know."

"Exactly so. In eyes we are as culpable as the killer himself. No doubt he has brooded on this during the years of mental anguish that he has suffered since, this 'temporary insanity' as Mr Johnson described it."

"Temporary!" I snorted, "the damnable fellow is clearly still insane."

"It would seem so, Watson. It may be that he had recovered to an extent, indeed he would have to have done so, to be in a position to take charge of Silas's affairs."

"But surely that is a ruse; his murderous intent is the reason he is here."

"I think not, it was triggered by an event of which, in a way, we unaware of although we were present."

"I am not sure I follow you."

"Henry Nanther was our companion for the train ride from Salisbury to Axminster. You no doubt recall his startled expression when you introduced me."

"Why, yes, but I attributed it at the time to other causes."

"That one moment brought back the one thing that had been exercising his diseased mind during his mental illness. I know all this is open to conjecture yet I see no great problem in so thinking."

"I thought he was looked familiar although I was certain I had never come across the man before. I caught no scent of 'Parisienne' cologne on the fellow though."

"No, but you no doubt noticed his dishevelled state, He rushed his toilet obviously and had not the time to liberally apply his cologne."

Matthew Johnson told us that Henry Nanther was staying in the old forge so laying hands on him should present no difficulty. I fully expected that Holmes would suggest that we arrest him with all due haste, I was therefore surprised that this course of action seemed to play no part in Holmes's plans.

"Thank you, Mr Johnson. When Inspector Baker puts in an appearance in the morning he can then have the privilege of taking Mr Nanther into custody and from there no doubt a swift return to the institution he has so recently vacated."

"Why not arrest the man now, Holmes, before he can do any more harm?"

"Even in his tortured state of mind he must know he cannot get to Legg, therefore his unfinished business is with me and I am most unlikely to come to any harm within the confines of this splendid hotel. The point is, he will not go anywhere until he has or attempts to have his revenge on me. In the meantime he will continue to reside at his brother's old house where Inspector Baker can find him at his leisure."

"And if he should choose to flee? What then?"

"Then he will be picked up by the Salisbury police on his return to that city."

"I have to say that I am not happy about it and nor I think would Sergeant Street and Constable Legg be so. Still, if that is your decision then I will abide by it, Holmes."

"Thank you, Watson."

Matthew Johnson excused himself, but before he could leave our company, Holmes stressed to him the importance of keeping his counsel on what he had learned tonight and he assured us that he would not be breathing a word to anyone.

I asked Holmes what had transpired between him and the officious naval committee and gave him, whether he desired it or not, the fruits of my own labours on the whole question of why Holmes had been brought down here.

"They are interesting points that you raise, Watson, your perspicacity has not left you entirely I feel."

"Thank you for the compliment, if indeed it was one!"

"Chamberlain took the floor for the meeting and gave it of his opinion that there was in fact no danger as regards the vessel being stolen and as for the presence of spies observing the trials, well, that

89

was neither here or there and could not be avoided anyway. I was in complete agreement with his words of course for these were precisely my own thoughts on the matter. His immediate concern was for the plans pertaining to the submarine now firmly ensconced in the safe here. He wished me to review the security arrangements that have been put in place and not only to review them, but to take full responsibility for the safeguarding of these precious plans. To that end he issued me with a key and advised that if anyone wished to consult the plans they could do so only by obtaining my permission to do so and in the case of my absence, that permission would have to be sought from Lord Walter Kerr."

"But surely the naval guard that are at present patrolling that floor of the hotel will still be doing so, the committee surely don't expect you to guard the safe day and night by yourself."

"Nothing quite as singular as that, but if Chamberlain thought he could arrange matters that way then undoubtedly he would have pressed it on me for he seemed unduly anxious."

"So you will be liaising with Lieutenant Webb I presume?"

"Yes indeed, one of those incidental pleasures that life is apt to throw one's way," he said, in a sarcastic yet genial manner. "Webb has been entrusted with a key also, it seems that part of his duties involve checking the contents of the safe periodically."

"How long do these trials continue for?"

"At the most, three more days, but probably less and believe me my dear fellow, notwithstanding your most agreeable company, I will be delighted to find myself once more in the seclusion of my Sussex haven. All the chicanery that is apt to attend on such affairs as this and those of, for instance, the affairs of 'The Second Stain', 'The Bruce-Partington plans' and 'The Naval Treaty' as you named them, quickly pall and becomes irksome."

"To those, I fear, we must add the tale of, 'The politician, the lighthouse and the trained cormorant'," I added, gravely.

"Now, that is one tale that must never see the light of day, Watson," Holmes admonished, sitting up sharply and fixing me with a searching look.

"I assure you I have no intention of laying that adventure before the public, Holmes."

"That is just as well for I fear none would believe it. The Admiralty would dearly love to hold more power than it does at present. They see themselves as the guardians of the people in no small part due to the successes and dominion of the Royal Navy although they are to some extent past glories and the recent history of the navy has certainly not been as glorious. They seek to be the clearing house for all official secrets and to run the network of agents and spies that have formerly been the province of others."

"This came from Mycroft?"

"Yes, there is no love lost between my brother and the Admiralty, he is considered old-hat and more than that, unnecessary in today's modern government."

"And yet they turned to him and thence to you when they needed help."

"Indeed, and it precisely that which is troubling me. What is really happening here?"

"The very question that was taxing my brain earlier, Holmes."

"So you have told me, but did you come up with an answer for that question?"

"Alas, no."

"Shall we have another?" he asked, pointing at my empty glass.

"I think not, Holmes, I have my orders! Do you intend to see Street tomorrow morning?"

"Yes, at first light and the leave the task of taking Henry Nanther into custody to the good Sergeant and Inspector Baker."

I put my empty glass on the table with the authoritative air of one who has decided enough spirits had been imbibed for the evening. Before I took my leave of my friend I made sure I had his assurance that he would not be taking any nocturnal exercise, particularly in the region of Ware Lane where a certain old blacksmith's forge was situated. He gave me his word that he would not dream of such an action which oddly enough, for I knew Holmes so well, did not reassure me in the slightest. Nevertheless I had no choice, but to take him at this word and I left him contemplating the dregs of his brandy and soda and made my way back to Coombe Street.

In the intervening interval, Angel seemed to have doubled in size and any hopes I had that this also implied a new maturity in the beast were dashed as my boots came under another vigorous attack as soon as I stepped over the threshold. I failed to see the attraction these boots held for the animal; I am quite confident that the boot-maker had not substituted a compound of aniseed for leather in the manufacturing process, thereby rendering them a veritable canine delicacy.

From the Assizes this week:

Joseph Tesoriere fined 8s for allowing his horse to bolt down Broad Street.

Sir Christopher Lovejoy fined the same amount for a public order offence.

Terence Grinter fined 7/6d for failing to deliver the mail on time in accordance with General Post Office guidelines.

Jonathan Routley fined 4s for breaking a window at the Volunteer Arms.

Geoffrey Baker and Peter Hackett fined 10/6d apiece and bound over to keep the peace for a year for engaging in a public brawl at the same premises.

Miss Allen and Mrs Colston fined 4s for using vile words in public.

Chapter Twelve

I rose early as was my custom of late yet even so found Nathaniel up and in the kitchen brewing a pot of tea. I furtively looked around.

"Don't worry; Angel is in the yard although it's about time I let her in."

"I am sure she will benefit from an extended period of fresh air!" although I was not being as altruistic as it may have appeared. "More gardening today for you, Nathaniel?"

"Yes and it looks to be a very warm spring day too. I am working for the Evans family in Sherborne Lane, a very small plot, but the wages are good. Have you and mother made any plans for today?"

"No, not that I am aware, although of course she may have done so and not informed me as yet!"

I informed Nathaniel how we had learned the identity of Legg's attacker and further how it was expected that Inspector Baker and Sergeant Street would be making the arrest that morning. As to Holmes's plans I could not enlighten him. He appeared to be solely at the mercy and whims of the Admiralty. I opened the door and took one step into the small garden where I planned to smoke a pipe in peace, then suddenly remembering the beast without, decided that once again discretion was the better part of valour and I beat a hasty and a somewhat undignified retreat.

Gradually, the kitchen and parlour became full of human activity as the rest of the household made their entrance. After a spell of twenty minutes of hustling and bustling in the confines of the small kitchen, breakfast was deemed to be ready. An honest English breakfast, simple fare perhaps, but nourishing and enough to set up the weakest of constitutions for the day. Beatrice and Elizabeth had not devised any kind of programme for the day, save for Elizabeth wanting to take Angel for a long walk. My suggestion that she took him as far she could and leave her to arrange her own return journey was met with a stony silence. It was entirely possible that my, as I thought, winning smile did not entirely disguise a certain intent on my part. Beatrice and I decided on a walk along the seafront a little later in the morning, allowing time for Elizabeth to perform her canine duties and return.....with the dog!

As always when Sherlock Holmes was in the vicinity, these arrangements were subject to change and so it proved to be. I was a little restless, a state that Beatrice could hardly have failed to notice. At her suggestion we wandered the few yards to Doctor Jacob's house and surgery to visit, we hoped, a still recovering John Legg. The surgery had just admitted its first patients of the day or to be more exact, just the one patient was in attendance. I nodded to Jacobs as he beckoned this patient of his into his inner sanctum and we carried on through to rear of the house where Legg was comfortably ensconced. Sarah was just leaving the room as we arrived outside it; the two empty plates were testament to a healthy appetite.

"Good morning, as you can see, our patient is doing much better and if he is here for much longer he will eat us out of house and home!"

"That is good news, Sarah," said Beatrice. "Has Margaret returned yet?"

"No, not as yet, I think the news would have only reached her this morning."

"We will only stay with a few minutes, he still needs his rest," I said, as we stepped over the threshold.

"His rest has been disturbed already, Doctor Watson. Joe Street and Mr Holmes were here some thirty minutes ago and they had a police inspector from Bridport with them. They were only with John for five minutes however."

"They had some news to impart to him; it is almost certain that our young friend's assailant will be in custody very shortly," I informed her.

"That is very good news indeed," replied Sarah.

John Legg was sitting up in the bed looking as hale and hearty as anyone could who had just survived a blow to the head and a knife to the chest. He gave us a welcoming smile and patted the bed, inviting us to sit.

"Good morning," he beamed.

"I have known many policemen in my time, some of them buoyant and cheerful in spite of the difficulties associated with their jobs, but I am sure I have never come across one as irrepressibly jocund as yourself. The manner of the attack on you would have left many men dispirited in the extreme," I stated.

"I see no gain to be had from that, Doctor. I am alive, I have my Beth, I do not consider myself hard done by. I did not become a policeman believing it would be an easy life, although at times it can be. I wanted to serve this community and as the saying goes, I must be prepared to take the rough with the smooth."

"You display great spirit, my friend. Is young Beth visiting this morning?"

"A little later I think; she is working this morning."

"What position does she hold?" Beatrice asked.

"She works at the small confectionary shop at the bottom of Broad Street, the small shop that faces out to the Victoria Hall."

The shop was familiar to me, for it sold in addition to confectionary, a range of tobacco including some I favoured and a few books pertaining to the history of Lyme Regis. The shop formed part of a Tudor building which had managed to escape the various conflagrations which were prone to sweeping through the town. I had noticed a new range of goods available to the public on my last visit; buckets, spades and fishing nets for children.

"Well, we will leave you in peace, you have everything you need?" I asked.

"Yes thank you, Doctor, I do and if not, look, I have a little bell here," he said, pointing at the bedside table, "one ring and Dr Jacobs or Mrs Jacobs comes running!"

"Don't overdo it, John," said a laughing Beatrice, "or you might find yourself home sooner than you think."

Rather than going straight back to Coombe Street to wait for Elizabeth, we elected to have a stroll. We took the path which meandered to the side of St Michael's church, through the small graveyard to the point beyond which afforded such wonderful views of the bay. In the distance we see the assorted vessels which made up the Navy's flotilla, although there seemed to be little by way of activity going on. The sun was rising steadily and the view ahead brought with it a certain uplifting quality which eased the soul. Lyme coming to life in the splendour of a sun-lit day was a perfect sight that positively demanded that you bask in its unblemished state. We retraced our steps and ambled down Church Street, passing the newly-built, but sadly empty museum, built incidentally on the site of Mary Anning's house. We saw Miss Markey on the steps of the shop she worked in and gave her a cheery wave before turning into Coombe Street. We met Elizabeth at the junction with Monmouth Street. Angel, I was gratified to see, was firmly attached to a lead, but the warmth of her, I presumed, pleasure in seeing me nearly brought Elizabeth to her knees. I idly speculated on removing the boots of mine that Angel was so enamoured of and running to the sea, hurling them beneath the brine with an enthusiastic shout of, "Fetch!"

Once we had treated ourselves to a welcome brew and 'caged' the beast, we wandered back towards the seafront. Holiday makers, who seemed to have an innate sense of when the weather would be perfect, were thronging the beaches and 'The Walk'. Families mingled with solitary walkers as they promenaded.

A sunny day in Lyme means a kaleidoscope of colour with a bright, azure sky which almost seems to touch the glinting, blue sea; the people who populate the seafront bring their own dashes of colour to bear on the scene. The scene is never constant; it is forever changing, moving and re-forming in this kaleidoscope of colour between the far horizon and the dramatic coastline of the bay. There are not many sights in my experience to challenge it; there is a sense that Lyme enjoying itself is life enjoying itself.

One of the figures ahead resolved itself into the form of Sherlock Holmes.

"Good morning, Holmes."

97

"Good morning, Watson and Mrs Watson, a pleasant one is it not?"

"Indeed. What news regarding the arrest of Henry Nanther?"

"Inspector Baker, a most congenial, amiable man and a far cry from the vicissitudes of the unlamented Baddeley, together with Street have marched off to Ware Lane on their official duty. I have no doubt we will hear very shortly the outcome of that duty."

At that juncture, the sound of running footsteps coming our way caused us to turn our heads. I felt a momentary alarm and instinctively thrust my hand into my pocket for the reassuring feel of my service revolver failing to recall it was still in my luggage. Alarm turned to panic and then to comparative relief at the sight of Lieutenant Webb.

"Good morning, Mr Holmes," said an out of breath and somewhat agitated Webb, "and good morning, Doctor, er, yes, good morning!"

"What can I do for you, Lieutenant?"

"The members of the committee wish to see you on a matter of the utmost urgency. Although of course they expressed it to me as an order, that is, to find you and bring you to them, sir"

"You have succeeded in the first part of your duties for you have clearly found me. Before, however, we can progress to fulfilling the second part of your edict, perhaps you could care to tell me what is troubling you?"

"I wasn't sure whether my course of action was correct, sir. Was I justified or not? That's the question I am asking myself. But, it's done now, but even so."

"It may be the question you are asking yourself, Lieutenant, but do not be too slow in asking me, for I have not the slightest notion to what you are referring."

"Sorry, sir, let me explain," he replied.

"Yes, please do," Holmes said, with increasing impatience in his voice.

"It's like this; after I saw you yesterday evening and we had discussed the new arrangements as regards the guarding of the safe and," here he lowered his voice, looking at Beatrice and me with an appreciable amount of suspicion, "I relieved one of the cadets under

98

me and took my position. Admiral Chamberlain called out to me from his room, which is on the same floor as the room with the safe. Are you with me?"

"As if I was there! Pray, continue."

"The Admiral's wardrobe had toppled over and I lent a hand to bring it back to a standing position. He asked me to stay in the room to hold it in position to prevent it falling once more and he would fetch the night porter to see if he could effect a temporary repair to the doors which were now hanging off."

"Were the doors hanging off a result of your exertions or as a result of the wardrobe falling?"

"They were hanging off when I entered the room; the wardrobe had fallen against the bed. There was a dim light in the room, but the corridor I had just vacated was brightly illuminated. There is a mirror by the door in the room and reflected in it I could see the Admiral removing a folder from his inner pocket. He knelt down by the safe, produced a key and opening it, he withdrew the papers for the new submarine. He removed a few sheaves and placed in this folder of his, put the rest of the papers back in the safe, locked it and disappeared out of view."

"That is very interesting. Now, you mentioned a course of action you took, please tell us what that consisted of."

"I ran into the corridor and looked down to the floor below where I could plainly see the Admiral going into the committee room and although I could not observe his actions, I distinctly heard the sound of a drawer opening and closing."

Holmes clapped his hands together excitedly, causing many heads to turn towards us.

"Excellent, Webb, you have covered yourself in glory. I assume your actions moved on from mere observance to some form of decisive activity."

"I was in a quandary for the Admiral is my commanding officer yet I could not square what I had seen with the position he held. If he needed to see some of the plans then he, like everyone, would have to go through the official channels to do so. Now, he may have had a very good reason for the clandestine action he took, but my brief was to guard the safe and its contents, not a duty I was about to take lightly."

"What did you do, Lieutenant?" I asked, unable to keep silent.

"I located the folder in the desk and removed the papers from it. There was a small pile of brochures in a recess, sir, I gathered a few of these up and slid them into the folder and replaced it in the desk drawer. When all was quiet, I opened the safe and restored the papers to their proper place. But even now, I think to myself, did I do the right thing?"

"Yes," said Holmes, "you acted for the best."

"But my career, sir, I may have ruined my prospects."

"We will see, I somehow doubt it. I take it the summons to find me came from the Admiral himself?"

"Yes, sir."

"Then we had best not disappoint the fellow. Watson, do you wish to observe what I think will be a most singular meeting?"

"I would like to, Holmes, but…"

"It's fine, John, Elizabeth and I will enjoy the spring sunshine together and we will see you *soon*."

"Yes, yes of course, my love."

"And do not forget I used the word, *soon*!"

The three of us turned against the tide of holiday makers and marched towards the Royal Lion, although truth be told, it was only young Webb doing the marching.

Reliable sources inform us that the Royal Navy trials currently taking place in the bay will be completed tomorrow. It will be most pleasing and beneficial for our local fishing fleet to have our waters returned to them. Having said that, we as a town are famed for our patriotism, and we are gladdened that the Admiralty saw fit to base so many of their senior officers in the town. Local hostelries have reported a thirty percent rise in the sales of rum!

We have had a lovely letter from Miss Lydia Hutchings (Printed in full on p13) in which she thanks us for our recent support of her venture. She also thanks the people of the town for coming out in huge numbers to support her and expresses the wish that not too many folk had been alarmed although we are not sure to what those remarks allude. Once again, we wish her every success for the future.

Chapter Thirteen

We left the sunlight of the morning and entered into the dimly-lit vestibule of the Royal Lion; its rich wooden panelling which created the atmosphere of the place also negated and thwarted most forms of illumination. Webb led the way upstairs to the inner sanctum of the Admiralty suite where we encountered a grim-faced committee.

Lord Walter Kerr gave me a cursory look, but said nothing regarding my presence there. Addressing Holmes, he said," Thank you for answering my summons. Admiral Chamberlain wishes to bring a most serious matter to your attention, Chamberlain…"

"Thank you. It is a most grave matter, Mr Holmes and sorry to say, it involves, I believe, a gross dereliction of duty on your part."

"Indeed, Admiral. I am most intrigued, pray continue," Holmes said, quite coolly.

"Your smile is misplaced, Mr Holmes, I assure you. I had enough confidence in your abilities, even allowing for the fact you are now retired, to put you in overall charge of guarding the plans of our new submarine. This, may I remind you, was only yesterday. Imagine my horror then, when I found some of those very papers in your room this morning, Mr Holmes. Have you an answer for this gross outrage?"

"I fear any answer of mine would be superfluous, Admiral."

"One wonders what you were planning to do with them. I believe we are looking at treason, no less."

"In my room you say? Where in my room?"

"It does not matter where they were," he blustered, "all that matters is that they were there at all."

"Which particular papers were they?" asked Lord Kerr.

"Oh, only the plans of the weaponry systems, nothing important," he replied in a sarcastic manner.

At this a collective groan went up from the members of the committee and Walter Kerr looked for the world as though he might burst a blood vessel.

"What have you to say for yourself, Mr Holmes? This is a grave charge indeed," asked Kerr.

"I was going to ask our esteemed Admiral whether he had the presence of mind to put these papers back in the safe. That is what I have to say at the moment."

"I have them here in this desk," he said, unlocking the left-hand drawer, "now what do you have to say? Perhaps you would care to give us *your* views, Mr Holmes," he said, with a sneer as he tossed the folder to Holmes.

Holmes caught the folder, looked at the contents, put them back in the folder and looked directly at Chamberlain.

"I personally find the Royal Lion Hotel a very fine establishment and these leaflets are excellent for the promotion of the services of the hotel. This kind of advertising I find works very well," Holmes replied, tossing the folder back to an apoplectic Chamberlain, "What do you think, Admiral? Perhaps you would care to give us *your* views."

The leaflets in the folder spilled out all over the desk as Holmes threw it back. Chamberlain pounced on them, searching through them desperately.

"But the papers were there, I know they were," he cried.

"Oh yes, Admiral, they were there, you are quite correct, but then, you yourself put them there. With your permission, mi'lord," Holmes said, addressing Kerr, he then shouted, "Lieutenant Webb, would you like to come and to your duty, young man?"

Webb hurried into the room, "Yes, of course, sir, but what duty?"

"Take Admiral Chamberlain into custody."

"Yes sir," responded Webb and taking hold of a still stunned Chamberlain, led him from the room.

"On what charge?" exploded the Admiral, "I have done nothing actionable."

The rest of his outburst went unheard as Webb manhandled him down the corridor.

"An explanation, if you will, of this extraordinary affair, Mr Holmes?" demanded Kerr.

"First of all let me say that the Admiral is most likely correct when he states he has done nothing actionable, nevertheless, I am sure he can be persuaded to resign as his actions have not been in line of those of an officer and a gentleman."

"Nothing actionable?" cried Kerr, "the devil you say, has he not stolen secret government papers? To my mind and that of any sane person, that is an actionable offence. Why, man it's treason, nothing more, nothing less. And where are the papers now? In the hands of foreign agents I wager."

"Calm yourself," soothed Holmes, "the papers are in the safe. It was never Chamberlain's intention to do more than borrow them for his own purposes. Passing them onto foreign powers would be anathema to him as much as it would be for any of you."

"Then why did he need them? Why accuse you of a theft that had never actually occurred," asked Richard Elkin.

"His wishing to discredit me was incidental to his prime motivation, which was to discredit my brother, Mycroft and bring about an end to his illustrious government career. He is pathologically jealous of the power my brother has yielded over the years and wanted that power, not just for himself, but for the Admiralty," Holmes replied.

"Yet it was his idea as I understand it, to approach your brother and request your services," said Elkin.

"For the reasons I have just stated," snapped Holmes impatiently. "You may not be aware, gentlemen, but John Chamberlain was a member of the Diogenes Club, that odd institution that my brother assisted in founding. There was, shall we say, a small scandal involving cheating at cards; my brother accused Chamberlain in no uncertain terms of being unworthy to be a member of that select body of men and the Admiral was forced to resign. The animosity he already felt towards Mycroft was heightened, resulting in what we have seen here today."

"How was it, Mr Holmes, that you came to know of his actions of last night?" asked Kerr.

"For that we must thank Lieutenant Webb for his watchfulness and perspicacity," Holmes replied and went on to explain in detail what the young Lieutenant witnessed and how he brought it to his attention.

The committee expressed their concern that in their view Webb should have approached them, but Holmes countered this by saying that when it came down to it, Webb did not know who he could trust.

"He did the right thing, gentlemen," he stated.

"On behalf of all of us, Mr Holmes, we thank you and feel we should apologise for you being here under false pretences, unless you feel there are spies……er……out there!" said Kerr.

"The whole area may be festooned with spies and agents, why not leave them to it? They will gain nothing from mere observance after all. If that is all, gentlemen, Dr Watson and I will wish you good-day."

"The ghost has been laid to rest, the Admiralty's problems laid to rest, let's hope Henry Nanther and his murderous intent has been laid to rest also, Holmes," I said as we walked down the staircase to the floor below.

"Amen to that."

"That's odd," I remarked, "what is that peculiar smell?"

I had no time to ponder further for a blow to the head rendered me senseless for a few seconds. When I looked up, I could see Henry Nanther holding Holmes with one arm around his neck and in the other hand, a knife which he held to Holmes's throat. I tried desperately to get to my feet, but before I could do so, Nanther had dragged Holmes into the nearest room and with a click I heard the key turn in the lock. Unsteady as I was when I regained my feet, I threw myself at the door, but to no avail, the door was sturdy enough to repel all my attempts to batter it down. My throat was dry with fear, but my shouts, weak as they seemed to me, brought forth Lieutenant Webb.

Together we attacked the door repeatedly, but all we had to show for our troubles was a splintered door frame. All was remarkably quiet in the room as far as we could ascertain and to be truthful, I feared the worst.

Then came a solitary click as the key was turned into the lock and the door began to open. We both stood back and prepared to spring at our foe. Joyously, it was Sherlock Holmes who appeared, smoothing back his ruffled hair. Peering inside, we could see the prostrate, dazed figure of Henry Nanther stretched out on the carpet.

"A most uncommunicative, taciturn man, Mr Nanther. I was attempting to explain to him the workings of the Japanese style of wrestling, baritsu, yet having elicited nothing by way of an intelligible response I decided a practical demonstration was called for, with the results you observe," waving a hand in the direction of the stricken man. "Could I call on you one more time, Lieutenant? A visit to the police house should find Inspector Baker and Sergeant Street. I am sure they will be only too delighted to come and retrieve Mr Nanther."

A few minutes later Inspector Baker and Joe Street arrived and took the still dazed Henry Nanther away.

"All our trials seem to be over, Holmes. Perhaps we can now enjoy fully the time we have left in Lyme."

We walked together from the gloom of the hotel to the sunshine of the day and set off in a leisurely pursuit of Beatrice and Elizabeth.

Later on that afternoon, we had word from Sarah Jacobs that John Legg and Beth Markey had announced a day for their nuptials and to help them celebrate, Sarah was planning an evening meal to which we were all invited. We were glad to attend and share this good news with them.

Beatrice, Nathaniel, Elizabeth and I wandered up to Monmouth Street for eight o' clock. Holmes had one or two points to go over with the naval committee, but he assured us he would be there very soon afterwards. Making her way up the lower part of Coombe Street we encountered Lydia, also bound for the Jacob's where we also found Joe and Belinda Street.

John Legg and Beth Markey were radiant in their full and complete happiness; although I advised the young constable not to overdo things for his recovery from his wounds was by no means complete. Holmes rushed in twenty minutes after eight, muttering away to himself.

"What's that, Holmes?" I asked

"I have just seen Mary Anning's ghost," he stated, "or of course as we know her, Lydia! I told her she had to stop; why she seeks to prolong this now her show is over I do not know."

"Good evening, Mr Holmes," announced Lydia, "you were saying? Was it something about having excluded the impossible, whatever remains, however improbable must be the truth?" she laughed, devilry in her eyes.

We all laughed with her as Holmes stood there looking dumbstruck.

"I find myself doubting the evidence of my own eyes," he said.

"Oh well, Mr Holmes, life can be strange," said Dr Jacobs.

"It can be unusual," added Beatrice.

"Often peculiar," I interjected.

"Inexplicable," added Street.

"Even grotesque," said Legg.

"Bizarre," said Beth.

"Fanciful," said Belinda.

"Singular," interjected Sarah

"Come now," urged Lydia, "we all know what it is don't we?"

"Yes," we chorused, "life is good."

Postscript

The coffee was poured. They talked presents and weddings with John and Beth. 'Thank you,' said Beth, 'I feel as though I have known you all for a long time.' 'That's what life is all about,' said someone else. 'Yes it is,' said Beatrice. Doctor Watson nodded in agreement and smiled. Sherlock Holmes agreed, 'ghosts need not apply'. Lydia beamed at him. Somewhere a dog barked. Nathaniel opened another bottle of wine and toasted the   happy   couple. 'Shall we toast Lyme too?' asked Doctor Jacobs. 'Oh yes,' said Sarah and they did so. 'No plum puddings this time then, Uncle John?' asked Elizabeth. 'No, sadly,' said Watson. The wine went around again and Lydia said, 'To us!" More smiles, more laughs. Lyme Regis never felt better to any of them then it did that evening. Joe Street together with his wife, Belinda told a story nobody understood, but they all laughed and went home happy and that's about it really.

The Grosvenor Square Furniture Van

This account of the affair, which had its origins in Holmes's looking into the mystery surrounding the Grosvenor Square furniture van, has been written with the help of Holmes, who aided me in filling up some of the gaps in my narrative for there were times when I was truly not myself and I had a voice which was not my own.

"Curse this thing!" I exclaimed one morning.

Sherlock Holmes, who at that point, was thoroughly immersed in the morning's newspapers and had not stirred for some three hours or more, now looked up.

"What thing, my dear fellow, and why curse it?"

"This writing-desk of mine; one of the legs is prone to giving way at the most inopportune moments."

"Perhaps a repair of some kind may be in order."

"That had occurred to me also, Holmes, and I have endeavoured to do so, but to no avail. I will just have to soldier on."

Holmes had nothing more to offer on the subject so he resumed his perusal of the day's news whilst I resumed my chronicling. The sound of running feet down below on the pavement followed by the clanging of the bell heralded the arrival of the telegram-boy from Wigmore Street Post office. Mrs Hudson duly delivered the missive and with a muttered, 'thank you' Holmes snatched it from her and tore it open.

"From Lestrade," he announced, "Not so much a crime as a puzzling happenstance it seems. He wonders if we would care to join him in Grosvenor Square, on the north side near its junction with Duke Street. What say you, Watson, do you fancy a stroll down to take a look at this riddle?"

"I think not, if it's all the same to you, Holmes. I do need to get these notes down today as goodness knows when I will next get the opportunity to do so."

"Very well, Watson," he said, donning his coat, "I will have a wander down and see how I may assist our old friend."

I had no reason to take an especial account of the time, but it was in the region of two hours before Holmes returned.

"Solved, Holmes?" I queried laconically.

"There was no crime to speak of just as Lestrade intimated hence there is no solution. All the same, it was and I daresay will remain quite a pretty problem. If you have a few minutes to spare me, Watson, I could run over the salient points for you."

With a sigh and an air of defeat, I put the cap back on my ink bottle and laid my pen and paper down.

"If you feel I could be of any help, then please do so."

"You will be of help my dear fellow by just sitting there and listening to my thoughts finding their voice. The commotion in the square concerned a furniture van which is owned and operated by Bradbury and sons of Mile End Road. The driver and his mate, namely, William Robinson and Jim Hodges, were nearly at their destination, which was the home of the Abernetty family in South Audley Street, when they heard an almighty crash from the interior of the van. Now, they also told me that they both had the impression that there had been other noises emanating from the van during the course of the journey, but these they attributed to the strapping coming loose which was supposedly keeping the furniture secure. They pulled up the horses and went to investigate. Imagine their surprise, Watson, on finding nearly all the furniture destroyed!"

"Had they been transporting a madman in their midst?"

"It was highly unlikely they had been transporting anyone for the doors of the van were securely locked when they left the warehouse in Mile End Road."

"What of it, Holmes? Locks are made to be broken, as you know only too well. Someone gained entrance to the van en route and set about destroying the furniture for reasons of his own. Maybe a former owner of the furniture? Or perhaps someone with a grudge against the Abernetty family?"

"I agree with you that locks are indeed made to be broken, but the only problem with your otherwise fine theory is that when

110

Robinson and Hodges went to investigate they found the lock on the doors secure, exactly how it had been at the commencement of their journey."

"I could advance you another theory, Holmes."

"By all means, let's hear it, my boy!"

"It's possible is it not that someone at the warehouse gained admittance to the van and hid amongst the furniture, thus when the doors were locked our culprit was already in place."

"Pray tell me, where this man of yours went for he was not in the van when the doors were opened on to that scene of vandalism."

"Hiding again, either hidden in the debris or behind other pieces of furniture for you did say that not all the furniture was destroyed."

"Another fine theory, but alas one that does not stand up to scrutiny. The debris was too fine for anyone to attempt to conceal themselves in such fashion. These pieces were almost totally destroyed and the only piece to remain unscathed was a bureau. This, oddly enough, was in the centre of the van with the remnants of its fellows strewn out around it and as such of course could not be used as a hiding place. Besides, if someone had been clever enough to conceal themselves how would they then effect an escape without being seen?"

"Was there any means of escape through the floor?"

"An intriguing thought which had occurred to me also. It did not seem that way I have to admit, but I can see no other way it could be achieved."

"Well, Holmes," I said, "When you have eliminated the impossible, whatever remains, however improbable, must be the truth."

"I fear in this instance that both the impossible and the improbable have been eliminated. The destruction met out must have resulted in a considerable noise and yet the drivers heard nothing to warrant them stopping the van until that last moment. Further, there are scorch marks amongst the wreckage yet neither man smelled burning."

"Perhaps this driver and his mate are responsible themselves, that may prove to be the solution."

111

"How could they be so? They could hardly come to a halt in the midst of heavy traffic and proceed to hack the furniture to pieces, surely someone, a good citizen, would be bound to inquire what on earth they were doing?"

"They could have done so in a quiet area or a deserted warehouse they knew of."

"That does not square with two facts I have in my possession. The time they left Mile End Road is logged and also the time of their arrival in Grosvenor Square, for having discovered the damage they hailed a passing constable immediately. There is no margin in the journey time for them to have made a stop of any kind."

"And the other fact?"

"I saw the men, they were still considerably shaken by what had happened and unless they both are accomplished actors I have to absolve them of any wrongdoing."

"The whole thing is impossible then, Holmes."

"I would have to concur with you yet I will give it some thought as I smoke, but I fear come the morrow I will have nothing to report to Bradbury and sons."

The matter rested there and when the morning came Holmes could still offer no solution to this most inexplicable of events. I had matters to tend to in town so we shared a cab as far as Aldgate where I alighted and Holmes continued his journey to Mile End Road where he would be the bearer of bad tidings. Still, I reasoned that the goods would have been insured while in transit, the Abernetty's would presumably have their monies refunded and if there was any justice, the driver and his mate would keep their employ.

After concluding my business I met up with Thurston for a game of billiards which turned into several games. Lunch came and went as did a bottle of wine and to clear the air and my head I took a leisurely stroll back to Baker Street.

Holmes opened the door of the sitting-room in what I could only call a state of exuberance.

"My dear fellow, I had almost given you up. I have taken certain matters into my own hands and I hope the result will be pleasing to you. Regard!"

He pointed in the direction of the corner of the room by the left-hand window, my corner. In place of my old rickety writing-desk, now stood a fine looking bureau, gleaming as though it had just been polished. A rich, dark brown gem of a desk.

"I can see you are puzzled, Watson. This handsome desk comes courtesy of Bradbury and sons. It seems the Abernetty family had no use for it, believing it must have been damaged to some extent. Oh, I have no doubt that Bradbury's will claim the insurance money for this bureau, but I am sure you will join with me in turning a blind eye to that particular infringement. They transported it here some thirty minutes ago and removed your old desk. I took the liberty of removing your papers, note-pads, pens and ink and deposited them in your desk in much the same order as they were in your old one."

"Thank you, Holmes. It's a wonderful piece and you have arranged my things on it to perfection, excepting of course the ink bottle. You have placed it on the left, not on the right where I have it."

Holmes followed my glance and then looked at me quizzically. The ink bottle *was* on the right, where he *had* placed it. I coughed an apology and blamed the wine and a trick of the light yet it had seemed so clear, so very definitely there. I shook my head and reprimanded myself for my thoughts.

The next morning found us in our customary positions. I with my pen in hand and Holmes seated by the fire with the morning papers scattered around him. I marshalled my thoughts and put pen to paper. I glanced at the desk in admiration as I wrote, it was so well made as to be a work of art yet I sensed, as strange as it seemed, that this bureau was somehow hostile to me. I do not have an overly sensitive nature and I could not account for this feeling. Dipping my pen, I wrote on.

It moved, it couldn't.

"Did you say something, Watson?"

113

"No, at least I don't think so, but the oddest thing has just happened, the desk moved."

"Moved? Like the leg of its predecessor?"

"No, it seemed to me it moved forward a fraction or lifted. I don't know, it was very fleeting."

"Are you sure it wasn't you nodding off, Watson, which caused this illusion? My impression was at breakfast that you are very tired indeed."

"I did not sleep well, I do know that. And when I did gain sleep I was caught up in peculiar dreams which haunted my night."

"Put your pen down and come for a walk. How about Regent's Park? The air will do you good and will aid you in sleeping later."

"A capital idea, Holmes."

We dressed ourselves with one eye on the vagaries of the English weather for recent days had seen equal amounts of sunshine and rain, but with no clear indication of which would come when. We spent two hours thus, conversing on many subjects as we strolled. He was bright, eager and in excellent spirits, a mood which in his case alternated with fits of the blackest depression. We traversed the park and having found ourselves on Albany Street, we elected to partake of a coffee at a nearby establishment we both favoured at the southern end of the street.

Refreshed, we made our way back to Baker Street by way of Marylebone Road. The refreshment I felt was immediately negated by my sight of the bureau; I could not escape the feeling it was pushing me away. I could find no rational explanation for this, it was just a piece of furniture, it was not animate. If this carried on I would fear for my sanity, but, I told myself, perhaps it was yesterday's wine and my lack of sleep.

Holmes had one or two loose ends to attend to in regards to one of his recent cases and had calls to make at both the British Library and Scotland Yard. I read the papers listlessly and hardly took in what I read. I looked at the writing-desk repeatedly as though I was challenging it to try and repel me. Tired of the nonsense in my head, I sat at the desk in a determined manner and resolved to write one chapter before the clock chimed six. The wound in my leg was causing me no small amount of unease; to try and alleviate this I stretched it out against the legs on the left of the desk. A few moments later I was aware of a creeping movement as though something was crawling over my flesh. I looked down to see the shape of a hand, *underneath the material of my trousers.* I could feel the coarseness of the skin and fingernails like claws that dug into my skin as the hand crawled. I gave a cry of alarm and half-climbed, half-fell out of the chair.

I retreated to the dining-table, breathing heavily. I rolled up my trouser leg, but there were no marks on my skin. The sensation of touch had gone and even I would be ready to admit I had fallen asleep and imagined it, for the morning's tiredness was still with me. I approached the bureau somewhat gingerly and knelt down to examine the legs. They were perfectly normal; there were no blemishes or roughness to account for my initial reaction. I sank back into the chair and more through nervous exhaustion than actual tiredness, I slept.

It moved, it couldn't.

When I awoke, Holmes was back. I made up my mind instantly that I would not share my experience with him. I had no doubts he would be a sympathetic listener, but his diagnosis would be sleep, or if not, then I would be commanded to pull myself together. Perhaps it was exactly what I needed to do.

I broached the subject of the bureau in a roundabout way with Holmes.

""Did Bradbury and sons give you any indication as to where the writing-desk came from? Do they know its provenance?"

"They did not volunteer the information, nor did I ask. Is it of importance to you?"

"No great importance, no," I said, weakly, "I just thought it might be interesting to know its origins."

"I do have an appointment in the morning with one of London's more disreputable pawn-brokers in Whitechapel Road. It is, but a short walk to Mile End Road. Would you like me to make enquiries for you?"

"If it's not too much trouble, Holmes."

"Pah! My boy, it is no trouble at all."

"Thank you."

"Are you writing a little more after we have dined?"

I gave the desk a glance and shuddered. "No, I will carry on in the morning when I may have the appetite for it."

"I only ask because I was intending to indulge myself with a chemical experiment tonight and I had no wish to disturb your concentration."

"That being the case, I may elect to retire early with a good book for company."

"Or failing that, one of your interminable sea-faring adventures," he laughed.

I positioned my chair as we dined so as to avoid any visual contact with the desk. Holmes asked what was troubling me, but I assured him it was only lack of sleep, nothing more. He looked at me intently, but did not raise the subject again. A few minutes later he spoke again.

"I can see you must have been a little out of sorts when you were writing this afternoon," he said, indicating the desk.

"I have said as much, but what is it you see?" I said, resisting the temptation to turn and look at it myself.

"Your ink bottle, you have placed it on the left."

"I did no such thing, Holmes," and steeling myself to follow his glance, I could indeed see the bottle now on the left of the desk. "Good God," I blurted out, "am I going mad? I swear the bottle was in its usual position when I finished my writing."

"There is something you are not telling me, Watson, I have interrogated enough people in my time to know when things are being concealed."

Backed into a corner as I was, I felt the only course of action open to me was to tell Holmes exactly what had occurred this afternoon and then invite his ridicule for I knew that would be the end result. He listened in silence, fingers steepled together in front of his face.

116

"At least I know now your sudden interest as to the origins of this piece of furniture. I wonder though whether once you have that information, assuming I can obtain it, it will make any difference. Knowing where it was made or who owned it is going to make very little difference to your nightmares that now appear to come to you by day as well as night."

"I was awake, Holmes! If it was a nightmare, it was a living one."

"Can you be sure? Could you swear to it? The mind can play games with us, my dear fellow; it can make us imagine we see what is not there. You have worked with opiate users; you know full well how their dreams and visions are real to them."

"I am not a drug user nor do I think that three large glasses of Beaune yesterday is enough to make me see visions. As to your questions though, I suppose I would have to say in spite of my conviction to the contrary, that it is conceivable that I had succumbed to sleep and that absent-mindedly I moved the ink bottle when tidying up."

"Excellent, Watson, for once you acknowledge a problem, you can begin to work at its solution. A good night's rest should see you rise tomorrow with all your fears unfounded."

I read later than I had intended, but even so, my sleep was uncommonly deep and long. If I had dreams they did not register in my consciousness and I woke feeling better than I had for some little time. I opened the door to the sitting-room and looked over to the desk. All seemed resolutely normal and for the first time I was able to gaze on it without perturbations of any kind.

"Good morning, Watson. You are looking refreshed I see, perhaps I missed my calling and should have taken up doctoring instead as my prescription has worked wonders. I have saved some breakfast for you and there is plenty of coffee in the pot still. I fear I must leave you very shortly otherwise a certain party in Whitechapel Road will be questioning my punctuality."

"He obviously does not know you well as there is no punctuality to question!" I observed drily.

"Don't scald yourself on the coffee," he said, slapping my back as he made for the door.

After Mrs Hudson had cleared away the detritus of breakfast I idled away the time looking through 'The Times' which had just been delivered. Having disposed of the day's news I assembled my thoughts with the view to getting down on paper the chapter it had been my hope to complete yesterday. In my high spirits of the morning I felt capable of anything and looked forward to the task with enthusiasm. I prepared my paper and ink and settled myself in the chair. The case I was chronicling was that of a missing heir and a murdered schoolmaster, which I had entitled, '*The Adventure of the Priory School*'. My pen flowed over the paper almost as though it had a will of its own:

'We have had some dramatic entrances and exits upon our small stage at Baker Street, but I cannot recollect anything more sudden and startling than the first appearance of Thorneycroft Huxtable, M.A., Ph.D., etc. His card, which seemed too small to carry the weight of his academic distinctions, preceded him by a few seconds, and then he entered himself -- so large, so pompous, and so dignified that he was the very embodiment of self-possession and solidity. And yet his first action when the door had closed behind him was to stagger against the table, whence he slipped down upon the floor, and there was that majestic figure prostrate and insensible upon our bearskin hearthrug.'

I declared to myself that I was happy with that first paragraph and proceeded to read it through again. This, as far as I can recall, is what I read:

'Huxtable, that buffoon collapsed under his own gross corpulence when he passed over our threshold. His pomposity was laughable, this irritating ugly man. He looked like the remains of a beached up whale on our bearskin hearthrug, his blubber spreading in all directions. If I had a harpoon to hand I would have run him through and ended his miserable life. Holmes was full of concern, the man even placed a cushion under this abomination's head. There would have been more work for the harpoon for the hateful Holmes,

118

who I have played second fiddle to for far too long, for he would have suffered the same fate...stuck like a pig'.

I looked at the words with growing horror. Where had they come from? I know I had not written this yet there was the evidence I had done so in front of my eyes. Yet, yet, I saw the words flowing as I first wrote and they were the words I had in my mind. What gross trick had made them as I see them now? I loosened my collar and poured myself a brandy and gulped it down and with trembling hands lit myself a cigarette. I still held the paper in my hand and although I hardly dared to look, I gazed downwards. It read:

'We have had some dramatic entrances and exits upon our small stage at Baker Street, but I cannot recollect anything more sudden and startling than the first appearance of Thorneycroft Huxtable, M.A., Ph.D., etc. His card, which seemed too small to carry the weight of his academic distinctions, preceded him by a few seconds, and then he entered himself -- so large, so pompous, and so dignified that he was the very embodiment of self-possession and solidity. And yet his first action when the door had closed behind him was to stagger against the table, whence he slipped down upon the floor, and there was that majestic figure prostrate and insensible upon our bearskin hearthrug.'

My joy at this return to normality was short-lived for the piece of paper burst into flames and was consumed with a rapidity I hardly thought possible. I tried to reason that the obscene words I saw had never been there, yet knew they had. But so had the other opening paragraph, the one I intended to write, how could they have changed? Once more I questioned my sanity, the cornerstone of my being. The fact the paper burst into flames was easily dealt with I thought for was I not holding a lighted cigarette at the time; a thought that consoled me until I realised the flames had begun their life at the top edge of the left hand side of the paper as I held it in my left hand and the cigarette was in my right hand held at my side.

It moved, it couldn't.

119

I did no more writing that morning and not feeling up to venturing outside; I spent the morning in cogitating and pacing the room like a caged animal at the zoo. I had the extraordinary notion that the desk was mocking me, deriding me. Yet, I was drawn to it, the power it exercised over me was tangible and I did not have the weaponry to fight it. The rich panoply of life that went on in the street below always fascinated me, but now I paid it no heed. I cannot tell how long this state of affairs went on for, but the spell was finally broken by the sound of Holmes's voice.

"Watson, you look as though you have seen a ghost!"

"So I look dreadful do I?"

"Well, yes you do, come and sit down."

"Damn you, I'll sit down when I want and not before!" I shouted as I left the room, slamming the door behind me.

I woke up later in the day lying fully-clothed on my bed with no clear recollection of how I had got there. I idly wondered whether Holmes had returned and carried me up to my room. As my head cleared I could recall that Holmes had returned and I had the vague impression
that words had passed between us. I returned to the sitting-room where Holmes was in the act of lighting a pipe and he gave me a curt nod.

"Did we have words, Holmes? I cannot bring the scene clearly to mind, but that is the feeling I have."

"Words are soon mended, Watson, we have no need to dwell on the incident."

"Thank you, Holmes."

"Watson," he said softly, " I have taken the liberty of asking Dr Moore Agar, the Harley Street physician to call this evening with a view to examining you. I am concerned about you, old fellow, or I would not have taken this step without consulting you."

I felt a rage inside at this, but it remained deep within so I thanked Holmes for his concern, but this Dr Agar could go to hell as far as I was concerned. Another irrational thought amongst my rational ones. My mind seemed not my own to command, the wonder was that I could actually acknowledge it. I was drawn to the bureau by the irresistible force of its very being. If I sat down, what horrors would be visited upon me?

"I have the information you requested."

"What information?"

"You can't have forgotten already surely, it seemed most important to you at the time; the provenance of the bureau."

"Yes, yes, of course, what can you tell me?"

"As far as can be ascertained the bureau was built in 1649 by cabinet makers in Warwickshire. It was commissioned by a Sir Robert Tilney who lived at Alcester Hall. I have not had the time to delve very much into the history of the man, but the British Library threw up some interesting facts, if facts they are. He was a hated man in the vicinity; servants would come and go as he was determined to mistreat them all. I noted a few appearances at local assizes where no doubt his money and influence could be guaranteed to win the day against the lower classes. It was said he dabbled in the black arts, alchemy and so forth."

"Tales of cruelty attach themselves to this man, Watson, throughout the years. Eventually his excesses went beyond the pale and a team of local militia stormed the hall to arrest him for witchcraft, amongst other crimes. They found a scene of horror, Tilney had been experimenting on servants who had not escaped his clutches and according to notebooks found at the scene that were later burned, he had been trying to locate the essence of evil that he believed all men possessed. The half opened skulls and the dead, staring eyes of these poor wretches testified to the the thoroughness of their master. They found their man hunched over a writing desk, feverishly scribbling and some of the militia men swore that underneath the desk was a hideously deformed creature. They wasted no time in blowing Tilney's brains out, summary justice for a cruel man. As his body slumped to the floor, the creature underneath the desk vanished utterly. The body showed signs of Tilney's depravity; wild, unkempt hair and long, crooked fingernails which looked more like claws. The body was burned where it fell and from these accounts it can be gleaned that the body was consumed by the flames in a very short space of time and it was remarked on at the time that neither the carpet nor the bureau showed any signs of burning at all. A salutary

121

tale indeed, no doubt embellished in accord with Warwickshire superstitions."

"And what of the bureau?" I croaked, barely able to breathe.

"Passed from family to family, house to house. It appears never to have remained in one place for long."

"Why is it so accursedly hot in here, Holmes? Why have you built up the fire so much?"

"My friend, look I beseech you, the fire is not lit."

I was loosening my collar and I think I would have removed all my clothing had it not been for Holmes's restraining arms around me. I felt myself calming down and Holmes relaxed his grip. I slumped into the chair.

"Holmes," I whispered, "that desk is evil."

"No inanimate object can be called evil. You are ill, my dear fellow, there are no spirits trapped in your bureau wanting to possess you."

"But that story!"

"Hearsay, folklore even. Who is to say that the event happened as was recorded? It had already been decided that Tilney was a witch or warlock. No doubt to put the fear of God into the locals, the story of his demise was wildly exaggerated. I searched through the local burial register for Alcester. They revealed that a Sir Robert Tilney was buried on April 14th 1658, in consecrated ground. In consecrated ground, mark you, not something which would have been allowed to happen had he been guilty of the heinous crimes this account would have us believe. Interestingly enough there is no record of any other burials around that period which does tell us that were no servants to bury as the account would further have us believe."

The ringing of the bell brought us back from the 17th century and into the present. Mrs Hudson ushered in Dr Moore Agar and he ambled over to greet me.

The consultation took place in the privacy of my room and to this day I cannot recall anything that passed between us and as Holmes was obviously not present he has not been of any help in the recording of what took place. The outcome I do know for Holmes and I discussed it before I finally retired that night. I was to present myself at Dr Agar's Harley Street rooms at nine o' clock the following morning and be prepared to stay for several days while I was treated for a nervous disorder.

My dreams had returned and I had spent a twisted and tortured sleepless night. I still had enough of a feel for reality to know that my grip on it was ever-weakening. When I entered the sitting-room Holmes was seated at the bureau, running his hands over it.

"Take your filthy hands off my property at once," I shouted.

"Apologies, Watson, there is no need to take on so."

"Move away from it, move away from it," I screamed.

Holmes did as he was commanded and I sat myself down in the chair. There was a curious hissing from under the desk (so Holmes later informed me) and two claw-like hands reached out. Dear God, I heard it, I remember it still.

"Yes, yes," I said, answering its unheard command..

I recollect Holmes's voice somewhere in the distance imploring me to act.

"Act, yes, by thunder I will."

I leaned over to the fireplace and picked up one of the steel pokers and stood there facing Holmes like the madman I had become. The rage filled my soul and I scorned Holmes for his lack of fight.

"Come now, man, you are coward enough to touch my desk, but not me? In the name of your god, strike me and give me the pleasure of silencing your tongue forever in the name of mine."

Sherlock Holmes sprang forward, a poker in his hand also. I raised my arm to strike him, but a felt a stab of pain as his poker connected with the bureau. Pain, a searing pain, shot through me several times over as Holmes rained blow after blow upon the desk. The stench

of centuries filled the room as the desk wilted under that attack. As I slumped to the floor, I saw an ugly, dark mass underneath the desk that resembled a living being; as the splinters flew, it shrivelled with a hissing noise and finally was no more.

We spent the next hour in locating all the pieces we could find of that evil abomination and consigned them to the fire. Only when the very last splinter was consumed did we relax.

"If you are all right, Watson, I need to go out and send a wire."

123

"To whom?"

"To Dr Agar, letting him know that you will not need that appointment after all."

Needless to say the mystery of the Grosvenor Square furniture van was never satisfactorily explained. All that was many years ago now, but I find nowadays that I always compose my chronicles at the dining-table and I have a marked distaste for old writing-desks whenever I come across them.

Acknowledgements

'Sherlock Holmes and the Lyme Regis Trials' brings to an end the series of three books ('Sherlock Holmes and the Lyme Regis Horror' and 'Sherlock Holmes and the Lyme Regis Legacy' being the first and second in the series). There is a limit to how many times the detective and the good doctor can be brought to a peaceful town on the coast which only had a population of 2,500 or so in the late Victorian/early Edwardian era. That limit is three. They have been enormous fun to write and I need to acknowledge here assorted family, friends and residents of Lyme who have found themselves within the pages of the three novellas either by name, character or voice (disembodied or otherwise!) And they are: The beautiful Gill Stammers (who is writing her own Sherlock Holmes pastiche), Lydia Hutchings, Tracy Heidler, Shaun Grattan, Sue West, Belinda Bawden, Liz-Anne Bawden, Louise Allen, Phil Street, Maggie Legg, Rikey Austin, Leon Howe, Joe Tesoriere, Hugh Duncan, Anthony Hutchings, Melody Ruffle, Donna Chapman, Maurice Beviss, Harry Long, Tim Bell, Matt Johnson, Matt Webb, Beth Markey, Terry Grinter, Pete Hackett, Lee Glanvill, Michael Stammers, Carole Twynham, Glenn Willis, Terry Sage John Routley, Geoff Baker, Stephanie Colston, Chris Lovejoy, Brian Matravers, George Elkin and Josie Farmer.

Special thanks to David Nobbs, the creator of 'Reggie Perrin' and one of Britain's finest comic novelists, for allowing me to 'pinch' a paragraph from, 'The Death and Life of Reginald Perrin'.

My thanks to them and everyone who has supported me during the publication of these three slim volumes. I believed I found the perfect setting for Holmes and Watson in Lyme Regis, but all good things come to an end. So we will leave them there, at Dr Jacob's, having a grand old evening. And that's about it really.

David Ruffle Lyme Regis October2012

In a glorious collaboration with the #1 artist in Lyme Regis, Rikey Austin, David Ruffle has created that rare gem, a Sherlock Holmes children's book.

Star Rating: 5 stars out of 5
"This is a wonderful book that gets it right."
The Well Read Sherlockian

Also from David Ruffle

Two collections raising important funds for The Beacon Society –
promoting the use of the Sherlock Holmes canon in education around
the world. David brings together more than thirty Holmes writers
from around the world with these eclectic and fascinating collections.

Tales from the Strangers Room – Volumes 1 and 2

*"A wide ranging collection of Holmes stories (and poems) from
writers new to the genre. Some are very short admittedly, but all are
more than satisfactory in their own way. An authentic sounding
Watsonian voice pops up every now and again amongst these tales.
Almost like a Holmes equivalent of a pick and mix, something to suit
everyone. Bottom line though is that it's a fun read. If you like your
Holmes and Watson a little bit quirky, you will enjoy this collection"*
Effortless Enigma

"David Ruffle follows his entertaining volumes "Sherlock Holmes & the Lyme Regis Horror" and "Sherlock Holmes & the Lyme Regis Legacy" with this sweet, sad novella called "Holmes & Watson: End Peace" - the punning title doesn't really do it justice. Nearly fifteen years after his "last quiet talk" with Sherlock Holmes, Dr Watson lies motionless in a hospital bed, conversing with a visitor only he can sense. The narrative consists entirely of dialogue - a bold and remarkably successful choice."
Sherlock Holmes Society of London

Also from MX Publishing

New in 2012 [Novels unless stated]:

Sherlock Holmes and the Plague of Dracula – New Edition
Sherlock Holmes and The Adventure of The Jacobite Rose [Play]
Sherlock Holmes and The Whitechapel Vampire
Holmes Sweet Holmes
The Detective and The Woman: A Novel of Sherlock Holmes
Sherlock Holmes Tales From The Stranger's Room
The Sherlock Holmes Who's Who
Sherlock Holmes and The Dead Boer at Scotney Castle
A Professor Reflects on Sherlock Holmes [Essay Collection]
Sherlock Holmes and The Lyme Regis Legacy
Sherlock Holmes and The Discarded Cigarette [Short Novel]
Sherlock Holmes On The Air [Radio Plays]
Sherlock Holmes and The Murder at Lodore Falls
Anomalous: The Adventures of Sherlock Holmes
The Untold Adventures of Sherlock Holmes [Short Story Collection]
56 Sherlock Holmes Stories In 56 Days [Reviews]
The Many Watsons [Review of Dr Watson Actors]
Sherlock Holmes and The Edinburgh Haunting
Sherlock Holmes and The Missing Snowman [Childrens Book]
Barefoot On Baker Street
Sherlock Holmes and The Case of The Crystal Blue Bottle
Sherlock Holmes and The Element of Surprise [Short Novel]
The Hound of The Baskervilles [Play]
Sherlock Holmes and Young Winston: The Deadwood Stage
Sherlock Holmes and The Lyme Regis Trials [Short Novel]
Holmes and Watson End Peace [Short Novel]

and many more at www.mxpublishing.com

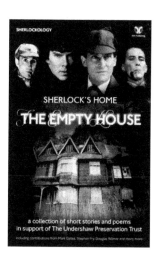

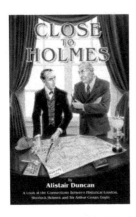

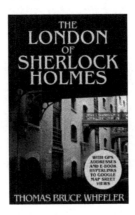

Also from MX Publishing

Sherlock Holmes Fiction

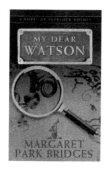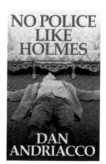

Short fiction (Discarded Cigarette, Russian Chessboard), modern novels (No Police Like Holmes), a female Sherlock Holmes (My Dear Watson) and the adventures of Mrs Watson (Sign of Fear, and Study in Crimson).

Biographies of Arthur Conan Doyle

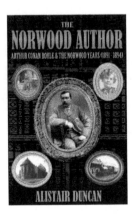 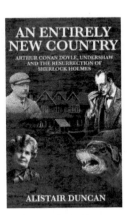

The Norwood Author. Winner of the 2011 Howlett Literary Award (Sherlock Holmes Book of the year) and the most important historical Holmes book of 2012 'An Entirely New Country'.

Also from MX Publishing

Cross over fiction featuring great villans from history

and military history Holmes thrillers

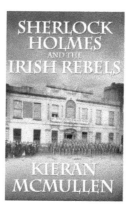

Also from MX Publishing

Fantasy Sherlock Holmes

And epic novels

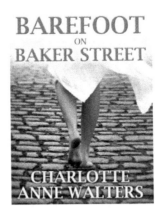

Also from MX Publishing

The first major Sherlock Holmes pastiche from an African American writer – Samuel Williams.

"Very few writers have tried to imagine what sort of things Sherlock Holmes got up to, and what sort of people he met during his years living as the disaffected Irish-American, Altamont, and infiltrating the Kaiser's spy network. He began his `pilgrimage' in Chicago, so it's natural that he would run into Diamond Jim Colosimo's criminal organisation and encounter one of its youngest members, Al Capone. Natural too that he would visit the Café de Champion on West 31st Street, to meet its famous owner, Jack Johnson, the first black world heavyweight champion. The great boxer is actually the central character in this powerful novel, by Samuel Williams Jr. Johnson's turbulent fortunes bring him to London, where two very different people, both black, have important roles to play in a struggle to save both Johnson's life and the security of the realm. "

Sherlock Holmes Society of London

A fascinating mystery that will test the skills of Sherlock Holmes to their utmost

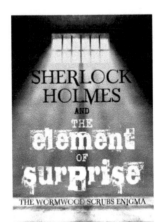

"*Now, this is how I like pastiches to be, namely on the short side with characterisations of Holmes and Watson spot on. To me very often less is more and here the author presents us with a novel crime which appears to be 'impossible' yet how can we think that with Sherlock Holmes on the scene. The plot development is skilful and not hurried along in spite of the brevity of the tale. The atmosphere is perfect and even the odd Americanism can be forgiven. I enjoyed this very much, but then as I have said it's exactly the kind of pastiche that does appeal to me. A big well-done to J. Andrew Taylor.*"
Effortless Enigma

A new collection of Sherlock Holmes stories from Save Undershaw
ambassador Luke Kuhns

*"This is a really good attempt to recreate the voice and magic of the
original Sherlock Holmes stories. The plots of each short story are the
true strength of this book and contain some very clever and
imaginative ideas. My particular favourite is The Adventure of St
Mary's Murder because I think that the deductions in this one are very
strong and Holmesian, for example (spoiler alert) 'The broken
window provided an interesting clue. We were told someone broke in,
though in all reality Leonora was trying to break out. Down on the
lawn lay hundreds of pieces of glass. Glass that, if someone was
trying to break into the church from the outside, would have fallen on
the floor of the sanctuary.' My only criticism would be that there are a
few typing errors scattered here-and-there, and at times the odd
phrase sounds a bit too contemporary but don't be put off by this - the
stories are great and I would highly recommend this book to any
Holmes fan. A very enjoyable read."*

Charlie221b